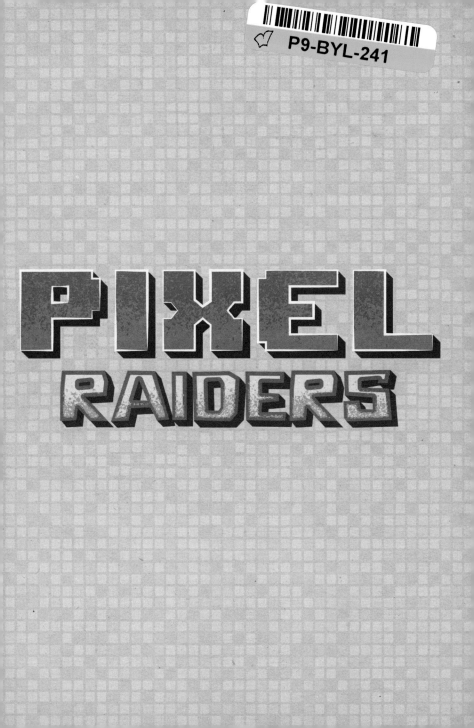

For our friend and mentor Janet "Sydski" Gaëta,
who created *Good Game* and *Good Game: Spawn
Point*. It is because of her that we began to share the
wonderful, imaginative world of video games with kids
(big and small) everywhere.—**S.B. + S.O.**

Rocketpig, to our games past, present, and future.—**C.K.**

Text copyright © 2016 by Stephanie Bendixsen and Steven O'Donnell
Illustrations copyright © 2016 by Chris Kennett

All rights reserved. Published by Scholastic Inc., *Publishers since 1920*,
557 Broadway, New York, NY 10012. SCHOLASTIC and associated logos are trademarks
and/or registered trademarks of Scholastic Inc.
This edition published under license from Scholastic Australia Pty Limited.
First published by Scholastic Australia Pty Limited in 2016.

The publisher does not have any control over and does not assume any
responsibility for author or third-party websites or their content.

ISBN 978-1-338-16118-2

10 9 8 7 6 5 4 3 2 1   18 19 20 21 22

Printed in the U.S.A.   40
First printing 2018

Book design by Baily Crawford

PIXEL RAIDERS

RAIDERS

DIG WORLD

BY STEPHANIE BENDIXSEN +
STEVEN O'DONNELL

ILLUSTRATED BY CHRIS KENNETT

SCHOLASTIC INC.

THE FLOOR IS LAVA

The gamer's skin prickled with heat as he leapt from stone to stone, narrowly avoiding glowing sparks of fire and popping explosions of molten rock. One false step and it would be GAME OVER. All he had to do was clear this platform section and make it to that narrow doorway, glowing bright atop the final stepping-stone.

There were several paths ahead.
Some of the rocks looked cracked and
unsteady. Others bobbed in and out
of the bubbling river of lava that
surrounded him. He would
only have one shot at
selecting the correct
stones to bear his
weight.

He waited as a boulder emerged momentarily from the molten river before leaping onto it, limbs flailing as he struggled to regain his balance. Immediately, he took another step, right before the boulder disappeared again beneath the lava's surface.

Beads of sweat started to appear all over his skin. The heat was fierce and distracting, making him dizzy.

Keep going. Don't stop!

He carefully selected the next set of stones and made a confident leap toward a large, flat rock that sat a little higher above the boiling river.

As soon as his foot touched down, he knew he'd chosen incorrectly. Something clicked beneath his boot—and his heart stopped.

He had barely a moment to turn and see the flaming arrow that had been triggered by the trap he'd stepped on before it plunged directly into his chest. White-hot heat engulfed him.

He opened his mouth to cry out, but he already

felt his body dissipating into pixels—and he had no voice to speak with.

Looking down, he saw his hands fading, shifting, pixelating—until they had blinked out of existence completely. This was it.

GAME OVER

He had failed. The burning, molten river continued to churn and surge against the rocks. The gamer waited to be taken back to the menu screen, so he could respawn and start again.

Nothing happened.

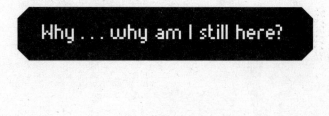

Why . . . why am I still here?

THINGS ARE ABOUT TO GET INREAL

Ripley stared at the digital alarm clock on his bedside table. **6:59**. He glared at the numbers from his pillow, willing them to tick over.

Any moment now . . .

7:00.
BLEEP! BLEEP! BLEE—

Ripley slammed a hand down onto the clock, silencing the alarm. He leapt out of bed with such a strong burst of excitement that his foot got caught in the sheets and he tripped, almost landing on his face.

"Whoa!" he yelped, relieved no one saw his first act of clumsiness for the day. He gathered himself up, catching sight of his disheveled and slightly red-faced reflection in the bedroom mirror. His features settled into an expression of fierce determination.

"Today's the day, Rip," he said to himself. He smoothed his hair over, trying to coax back the flattened part that always seemed to get stuck in the same position when he slept, making him look like he'd been caught in a windstorm.

Today was the day of the school field trip.

Like everyone else, Rip liked getting the chance to spend a day out of the classroom. But most field trips didn't really thrill him beyond that. They were more fun for the kids who were good at math or science or sports or music.

But Rip—he was one of the best gamers in the school. Everyone knew it, and it was something he was very proud of. So that's why this field trip was a BIG deal for Ripley. Today they would be visiting INREAL GAMES—one of the biggest gaming companies in the world.

They were responsible for all the greats:

TEAMFORCE SPLATTER
DUNGEONS OF DIREWORLD
Space Horizons 1, 2, 3, and 4

. . . and so many others. He couldn't *wait* to see the very place where all these games were made.

Besides, who knows? Maybe today he'd be able to take a peek at some secret, unannounced game that INREAL was working on. He could show off some of his skills, and they'd see what a dedicated, highly skilled gamer he was. "This kid has a bright future in video games!" they'd say. "Perhaps he should skip school altogether and come work for us!"

Caught up in the daydream, Rip quivered with glee at the thought. He hoped to create his own games for INREAL one day . . .

"RIPLEEEEYY. I DON'T HEAR THE SHOOOWEER."

Ripley snapped back to reality.

"SORRY, MOM!"

He fished around for his towel amid the messy chaos of his room, managing to retrieve it from beneath a pile of video-game boxes (none of which had the correct games in them).

No more time for daydreaming. Today, he absolutely would *not* be late.

Mei Lin grabbed the last empty seat on the school bus and plonked her schoolbag down next to her. *Perfect.* With no one next to her, she'd be able to just play on her portable gaming device without any fuss or interruptions. She liked it better that way.

Mei pulled out her Digi-Play and loaded up Dungeons of Direworld—it was her favorite, and she was on the second to last boss. So far, she hadn't been able to beat it, but she knew she was close.

As she waited for the level to load, she cast her eyes around the bus.

"Why haven't we left yet?" she asked one of the kids behind her. It was Angela, who had decided to start munching on her packed lunch already.

Angela shrugged. "I think we're still waiting for someone," she said, chewing with her mouth open. Seeing Mei's unimpressed reaction, she grinned. "Do you like see-food?"

She opened her mouth wide, giving a decent view of half-chewed peanut butter and jelly sandwich.

"Ugh. Gross, Angela." Mei scrunched up her face and turned back around to see Ripley standing alongside her seat and glaring at her.

Mei didn't know Ripley very well, but she knew he was a good gamer. She'd seen him posting his high scores and speedruns online, and some of them were better than hers. A *lot* better. It was annoying.

"I *said,* move your bag, *please."*

Mei begrudgingly pulled her bag off the seat and glared back at him. Rip sat down next to her and sighed. It looked like he'd just been running.

He shot a sideways glance at her. "I missed my train," he explained.

"Oh. So you're the reason we're going to be late to INREAL," Mei replied. "Thanks a lot."

Rip didn't say anything. He just folded his arms and stared ahead.

Mei went back to her game, letting her hair fall down over her face like a curtain to block out the world. Mei's hair was like her safety net. It was glossy and black, but she liked to clip a blue hairpiece into the front for a bit of a "punk vibe." She figured it made her look rebellious and people would be less likely to mess with her. Mei hit **start** on the console and the boss fight began almost immediately. She had only managed to get a few hits in, however, when she noticed Rip leaning over her.

"I know a better way to win that fight," Rip said, matter-of-factly.

Mei scowled slightly. "No, thanks. I want to figure it out for myself. Besides, I need the practice. I'm going to win the competition today."

Rip's heart almost stopped. "Competition? What competition?"

"Are you serious?" Mei's eyebrows went up in disbelief. "I assumed *you'd* be all over it. The contest being held at INREAL GAMES today between all the students. The gamer with the highest score will get to test out some new title they've been working on."

Rip's mouth fell open. A BETA test! That HE could be a part of? *How did he not know about this?!*

"It was on the permission slip," said Mei, as if reading his mind.

She went back to her Digi-Play, her fingers deftly skating across the buttons on the game pad.

He'd been so excited when he saw the words "FIELD TRIP" and "INREAL GAMES" that he hadn't even bothered to read the rest of the note. If he had known about a competition, he would have been putting in extra gaming hours to really get his skills up. He glanced nervously over at Mei.

The bus engine suddenly roared to life. Rip's mind was racing. This could be it. This could be the day that changed his life forever.

"HA!" Mei exclaimed, then blushed, clearly embarrassed that she'd been so loud. "Got 'im! See? Told you I could do it." She held up the Digi-Play casually, showing off her score.

She was good. *Curse it!!*

Rip sank down into the seat. If he didn't win the INREAL competition today, this could turn what was meant to be the best day of his life into the worst.

UN-FUN FACTORY

UNREAL GAMES was surrounded by a massive cement wall that seemed unusually tall. Surely this wasn't the game studio? Ripley and the other students were expecting an exciting, bustling fun factory, but this looked more like a prison.

They drove alongside the wall for what felt like hours until they reached a smooth, blue section which appeared to be the way in. There was a man with a clipboard, waving them down.

The bus came to a halt, the doors opening at the same time. The bus driver leaned her head down the aisle and barked, "EVERYBODY OUT!"

Rip leapt up, pushing past the other kids to exit the bus. Mei shook her head, and carefully powered down and packed up.

Rip stepped off the bus. He was sweating, and still panicking about the contest. "It's OK, Rip. You can do this," he mumbled. "Rely on your skills. You've been in competitions before. You've got this." He looked up to see Mei directly in front of him, staring.

"Do you talk to yourself a lot?" she asked.

"It helps me focus," he said, frowning.

"Please focus more quietly," Mei replied.

The man with the clipboard raised both of his hands up in the air and waited until everyone was quiet.

"Welcome, students," he said in a slow, monotone voice. "I am your INREAL GAMES tour guide. Before we enter, I need to go through the rules. We have many rules. Rules make our company work. Obey the rules and you will have a fun day. Disobey the rules and you will be removed and permanently banned from all INREAL games. Rule One, NO talking. Rule Two, follow me, in a single line, as soon as I stop talking. I will now stop talking."

The blue wall parted in the middle, opening inward and revealing a long, smooth tunnel. Clipboard Man walked through the doors, and everyone lined up and followed politely.

Rip moved behind Mei and nudged her. "Can you believe this guy is our tour guide?" he said. "You'd think that he'd be a bit more excited, you know, working in a video-game company and all."

Mei glanced at him. "He said no talking," she replied, and turned back around, walking at a slightly faster pace.

Soon the tunnel opened into a massive hall. The walls, ceiling, and floor were all made out of gray squares. The hall was filled with row after row of cubicles. They were gray too. The chairs were gray. The pens were gray. The computers were gray. Each desk had one mouse, one keyboard, and a computer. All gray. There was nothing else on them. No video-game boxes, no consoles, no controllers. Just rows of computers, desks, and chairs. This did *not* look like the sort of place where awesome games were made.

Rip knew that it took hundreds of people to make video games, especially games with the quality of INREAL GAMES titles. Where did the play testing happen? Where were the exciting conversations the developers were having, coming up with new game ideas?

For that matter, where were the people?

"Where is everyone?" Mei uttered quietly.

"Shh, no talking!" said Rip, mocking her.

Walking through the deserted hall, they all approached another large blue door, with TEST CHAMBER #10481337 printed on it in white. Clipboard Man raised both his arms high in the air again, and everyone shuffled to a halt. He turned around and said, "This is test chamber number 10481337. This is where you will be tested."

The group of students looked at one another uncomfortably. This was all happening very quickly.

Sam, a talkative boy, and also a bit of a class clown, put up his hand and started speaking straightaway. "Hey, I thought we were gonna get to play some games? There's enough tests at school. I came here to get OUT of tests."

A few of the students giggled.

Clipboard Man turned toward Sam. He wrote something on his clipboard. "Hello, Sam. You have broken Rule One, NO talking. This is an error," he said calmly.

Suddenly, the gray square below Sam glowed red. He looked down, puzzled. Without warning, it opened like a trapdoor, and Sam disappeared.

"Sam has gone to the waiting area. He will join you again on the bus home."

The kids looked startled. What was this place?

Clipboard Man continued. "When the door opens, you will have 4.2 minutes to find a chair, sit down, and start playing. There will be three different games for you to play today. Only the highest-skilled players will receive an invite to the BETA of our latest game, and get to help shape its future. If you do poorly in any game, you will not be invited to the BETA. You will not be involved in its creation. You will not be asked to participate in *any* future INREAL GAMES projects. Ever. Oh, and have . . ." He looked down at his clipboard. ". . . fun."

This wasn't feeling very fun to Rip.

Then the blue door creaked open and everyone charged in.

LET'S GET READY TO BUTTON MASH

Mei Lin stood gaping for a moment, before realizing the herd of kids had stampeded past her and she was now standing all alone. She blinked, snapping back to attention. Ripley was already at a console, putting his headset on.

There was an empty spot near Angela, who was with a group of her friends, giggling loudly at something. Mei didn't need that kind of distraction. Honestly, some people weren't even taking this seriously! Her eyes darted around the room. In the back corner, she spied a free console and made a run for it.

"Oh!" Mei cried as her foot caught on something, nearly sending her sprawling. She

collected herself and
looked back to see
what she'd tripped on.

"Oops." A kid called
Brayden was grinning
at her. He was an
annoying boy who
liked to play pranks on
people. *Mean* pranks. Sure
enough, Mei saw that he'd kicked his schoolbag
into her path as she was running. "Better be
careful, Gamer-Girl, or you won't win the big
awesome *nerd* prize!" He snickered, and his
friends joined in.

URGH. Really?! It certainly *wasn't* funny
to Mei.

"Yeah, you're so *hilarious*, Brayden," she fired
back sarcastically, trying to hide any sign of hurt
on her face.

You don't have time for this, she told herself,
focus on the game—that's why you're here!

Mei's lips set into a thin line of determination as she took her seat at the console and lifted the headset onto her ears. She logged into the INREAL system, creating a profile using her screen name: M31.

The other students' screen names appeared on a player list as the game loaded. She saw a screen name she recognized: RIP.

She grinned. "RIP" was also the initials for "Rest In Peace." *Nice one, Ripley.*

"The first battle will now begin," Clipboard Man said sternly. The blue door shut firmly behind him, closing everyone in. "By now you will have entered your screen names. However, for this test,

	INREAL GAMES ⊠
1	daRKFIREANGeL60
2	Crikeyboy
3	RIP
4	NooBZApper2001
5	rocketpiG05
6	SAUCEMAGNET
7	TimBOLtRon
8	RollerGRL_75
9	Rosiek2005
10	31_HeatH
11	stuRRY_P5
12	suzq
13	P1P_99
14	M31

you will not be able to see one another's screen names in-game. This is to ensure no alliances are formed, and that you are all relying on *individual skill* alone."

Angela raised her hand. "Um, what if I have to pee—"

"START!" Clipboard Man yelled.

Suddenly, the screen went black and the game began. Mei recognized it instantly. It was **space Horizons 4**—an aerial space laser-shooter.

Mei switched the flight-control settings to inverted, so she'd be using the thumb stick on the game pad like a *real* pilot would use a control column in a plane.

She launched the space fighter with fierce precision. Ship-flying games were not her biggest strength, but she'd played through all four editions of **space Horizons** and had developed some pretty crafty techniques.

ZOOM!

Mei turned, banked,
and wheeled her ship through
asteroid belts and zipped around planets.
She fired her ship's laser at space debris in her
path, seeking out other players' ships. One, two,
three . . . she zapped spacecraft out of the starry
sky with ease. Things were going well so far.

As Mei took down one fighter after another,
her confidence grew. Feeling bold, she performed

a series of clever acrobatic maneuvers with her fighter, and focused her sights on two of the remaining ships that were locked in a laser-fire battle with each other. Mei checked the game's heads-up display to see two heat-seeking missiles in her arsenal that she'd been saving. Now was the time to use them! Mei locked on to one of the ships—and fired! A moment later, the second missile was away, both seeking out their targets with deadly precision. A fiery pixel explosion reflected brilliant orange in Mei's eyes as both ships dissolved from existence, their players out of the game.

She heard a groan from the other side of the room. It sounded like Brayden. Mei couldn't help but smile.

Mei guided her spacecraft around the remaining debris, scanning the screen. All was quiet. Was this it? Had she actually won?! There were no other ships in sight. Mei performed a barrel roll to avoid an asteroid as she coasted toward a pretty red planet with rings around it, feeling a flood of relief. If the whole competition was going to be this easy, she would be the winner for sure.

But why wasn't the game over? Where was the score screen?

By the time Mei noticed the missile-lock, it was too late.

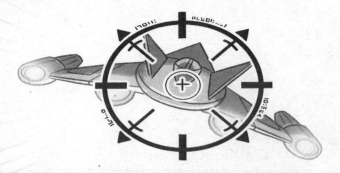

"YES!"

Rip couldn't help but let out a few fist pumps into the air as the words **GAME OVER** appeared and the score screen popped up with *his* name at the top. Rip stood up and looked over the row of monitors to where Mei was sitting, still staring at the obliterated ship on her screen in disbelief.

"Nice try! Maybe next time!" He waved at Mei playfully. That last stealth maneuver he'd pulled was nothing short of perfection. He'd won the game!

Mei looked at him with a mixture of anger and hurt on her face. "For you, there isn't going to *be* a next time," she said firmly.

Rip frowned and sat down. *Gee, what a sore loser!* He couldn't help it if he was the best gamer in the room. He perked up at the thought, wondering what kind of game the BETA title would be—since he was *obviously* going to be the one who got to play it.

Round two began almost immediately, with all the students back in the game.

SUPER BLOCK KNIGHTS was a melee sword-fighting game set around a battlefield at the foot of a huge castle. *Nice,* Rip thought. It was another game he was pretty familiar with and he felt sure he could repeat his success.

There were two classes to choose from:

KNIGHT   **ARCHER**

Rip chose Knight.

Generally he was better with ranged weapons, but in this case the heavily armored Knight with harder-hitting attacks seemed like the better choice to give him a competitive edge. He was

also equipped with a small shield. It would add weight to his character, slowing his movement, but the extra protection would be worth it.

3 . . . 2 . . . 1!

Rip urged his character forward, metal armor clanking as he ran.

His first opponent came charging straight for him; a Knight with a sword raised high above their head. It was an obvious attack, so Rip blocked the blow easily with his shield and then countered with a low strike.

Rip's sword knocked the Knight back with a stagger, leaving them open for another blow. Acting quickly, Rip launched into a final sword strike that saw his foe disappear in a shower of pixels.

Somewhere in the room, Angela could be heard wailing angrily.

His next few fights were a little tougher, as a large group of Knights and Archers had collected in some stone ruins and were locked in a group melee. As Rip approached, he lifted his shield in

front of him, and felt the frightening thud of arrows raining into it. He made a move toward a nearby Archer, but another Knight got there first, striking the Archer down. Rip then caught the Knight unawares, and with a single, swift blow they too disappeared into pixels.

It wasn't long before he was locked in a final one-on-one battle with an Archer, who had already sunk five arrows into his shield, and was loading another into their bow.

Rip grinned. This would be the moment.

Just as the Archer had loaded the next arrow, Rip's sword came down and another explosion of pixels saw his opponent out of the game.

Rip glanced around the pixel-laden battlefield. Swords, bows, and shields lay scattered everywhere. But the game wasn't over. There must be one more player left.

Suddenly he heard a noise behind him.

He whirled around quickly to see an Archer, perched high on a crumbling wall, with an arrow aimed right at him!

No! Before he could raise his shield, the arrow whizzed from its bowstring and struck his avatar in a devastating pixel-burst.

GAME OVER

How? How??! How could he let that happen? How could he have let himself become distracted at the very last moment—*the very moment when it mattered the most!*

The score screen flashed up and, sure enough, there it was. At the top of the list of players—**H31**. He looked up to see Mei peering over the monitors at him, grinning.

Rip's mind raced. He and Mei had both placed first and second in the last two rounds, giving them the highest scores. None of the other players in this group were even close to being competition—he was just too good. But apparently so was Mei!

Whoever won the next game—Rip or Mei—would have the overall highest score.

The next game would be . . . the *decider*.

DIVIDE AND CONQUER

Clipboard Man raised both arms in the air. "It's time for the third and final round. Remember, we are only looking for the most skilled players. Seven of you have done so badly in the first two games that you've already failed. Everyone put your controllers down and connect your keyboards please."

The stress of this competition was starting to get to Rip. Getting to play INREAL GAMES' next game *before* it was released was a big deal. He'd be the envy of everyone. But, if he missed out, other gamers from school, and those he played with online, might start to question his gaming skills. They could even go so far as to call him a "NOOB."

Rip was obviously not a NOOB.

NOOBs are gamers who are terrible at everything. And if you were branded a NOOB, you'd have to defend yourself online for the rest of your life!

Games were everything to Rip. He organized guilds on weekends where he would train new players. He read every review and followed every gaming channel online so he would always know what was coming out and when. He loved everything about games. He often dreamed of a day when games would look almost as good as real life.

If he didn't get into this BETA, it would be months—maybe even *years*—before he could experience whatever INREAL GAMES was cooking up. Rip was not willing to let that happen.

Clipboard Man lowered his arms. "The next game is **GLOBAL CONQUER**. Your goal is to defeat as many players as possible with your armies. Afterward you will be asked to leave and you will each receive a piece of fat-free turnip cake."

Turnip cake??
What on earth?

Rip shrugged, connected his keyboard, and waited for the game to load.

GLOBAL CONQUER was a complex strategy game where world leaders fight it out for total control of Earth. It required a combination of diplomacy, base building, resource management, and lots of attacking and defending. It was not a game just anyone could pick up and play and be good at. You had to practice to stand a chance online. You had to know all the units well and how to build them efficiently. Most of all, you had to know how to make a plan and execute it perfectly.

Mei smiled. It was right up her alley.

The screen blinked on and a blank patch of land appeared, with one single unit called a "Founder."

It was a tiny little pixelated family and their

pixelated horse. Soon her screen would be filled with a mighty army!

Mei prided herself on being prepared for games like this. She practiced over and over against the computer AI and only when she could beat it on the hardest difficulty, did she then feel ready to play against others. She always won. She was an unstoppable force of strategic domination on the battlefield.

Mei immediately started building a base of operations. She already knew exactly what she was going to do. Her strategy was all about "turtling." She would build strong walls around her base, put down a practical selection of turrets, and steadily build up her armies. Then, when the time was right, she would send them out as one giant, unbeatable force and conquer the entire planet. All she had to do was build, defend, and wait.

All Rip had to do was find Mei. He knew the only way he was going to stand a chance of winning today was if he could take out the biggest threat in the game world. Without a doubt, that would be Mei.

He flicked his mouse and keyboard around with the speed of a pro. "Where are you?" he said, squinting at the world map as his drones flew around.

He loved drones. They were cheap to produce and could scan huge areas of the earth to reveal enemy bases. His initial goal was to find the most advanced base on the board. That would be Mei's. Then he'd rush it with everything he had.

He flew past a few players fighting it out in a swamp with tanks. *They're using ground units in*

a SWAMP! he thought, shaking his head. Not only did this cut their movement speed in half, 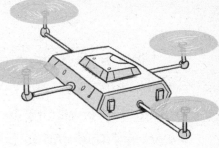 but they also took water damage and would rust within minutes.

"Amateurs."

If the rest of his class was playing this badly, he would have no problems dealing with their puny bases. But they weren't the concern right now. He had to find Mei.

One of Ripley's drones beeped, crackled, and crashed into the ground. It had been shot down in a wide green field next to one of the most well-defended bases that Rip had ever seen.

Triple walls. Golden turrets. And within those walls, a massive army of tanks and soldiers, just sitting there, waiting to be unleashed. It was glorious! This HAD to be Mei's base.

Rip had to act fast. He'd been building sniper jets with upgraded lasers since the start of the game. They weren't very tough, but they moved fast and packed a real punch. Rip clicked a few keys, and then the jets were on their way to Mei's base. He just hoped he had enough of them to breach her defenses.

The sniper jets came out of nowhere. Mei flicked her cursor around the screen, trying to rebuild her armies and repair her turrets, but every time she managed to get things fixed, another wave of sniper jets would come in and destroy it all again. She began to panic; she'd never had someone attack her base with this much force so early in the game. She sat up in her chair and looked around the room. Rip was grinning wildly. Of course it was HIM.

"UGH!" Mei got back to repairing her base.

Rip's rushing tactic was impulsive and impractical. The more time he spent attacking her base, the more time he would lose defending his own. It just wasn't a good strategy for this kind of game!

The tug-of-war battle with Rip went on and on. Mei couldn't get ahead, and Rip couldn't do enough damage to destroy her base entirely. They were going around in circles.

"No, no, no, no, no!" Rip screamed suddenly, frantically clicking at his keyboard. Alarms sounded as a massive army of copper tanks rolled into his base. He quickly called all his jets back, but it was too late. **CONQUERED** flashed up on the screen as his last building collapsed to the ground.

"NO!" Rip grabbed the computer screen with both hands, staring in disbelief. He'd made a fatal error. By spending all his time attacking Mei, he'd left himself

wide open to attack from the other students.
They had no trouble at all wiping out his relatively
small base. He looked up and checked the
scoreboard. Last. Rip was last. He'd never come
last in a game before. He felt sick.

Mei breathed a sigh of relief. With Rip out of the
game, she could get back to her plan. She was
just about to queue up some repairs, when
multiple armies of copper tanks rolled into view
from all sides of her base. There was nothing
she could do. Rip's last attack had destroyed
almost all her forces and left multiple holes in
her defensive walls.

She had lost too, and it was Rip's fault. She stood up and glared at him. He glared back, arms folded.

A few more shouts filled the room as the rest of the students finished off their game. Mei and Rip both stared at their screens, listening to all the other students rack up points, while they had none.

Then Angela leapt up and pointed back and forth between Rip and Mei. "YES! In your face, losers!"

Mei could see **CONQUEROR!** flashing on Angela's screen. She had won. She had conquered ten students. Mei and Rip had conquered none.

Clipboard Man raised both arms. "The games are over. I will now tally the total scores and read out the names of those who have been selected to join the INREAL GAMES BETA program. In first place, Angela. Second place, Timothy. Third place . . ." He went on to read another handful of names. "And finally, Brayden. If I did not call your name, you did not do well enough."

Mei's jaw dropped. Rip looked pale. It was official. They didn't get in. They'd failed.

Mei stood up and pointed at Rip. "YOU!" she shouted. Everyone was watching. "If you'd left me alone instead of harassing my base, we'd both have lots of points. You ruined everything!"

"Hey!" Rip replied, slightly embarrassed. "You were turtling; I had no choice!"

Mei walked closer. "You have to think of the bigger picture, Ripley! We were the best players in the room. Our plan should have been to get points by taking out the other players first, not to try and destroy each other. That was a waste of time. It was not a logical plan."

QUIET!

NO TALKING!

OBEY THE RULES!

Mei sat back down. Clipboard Man's face was red with anger. Then, suddenly, he was calm again and looked down at his clipboard. This guy was weird!

"Thank you for coming to the INREAL GAMES field trip day. Now line up in a straight line and follow me."

Clipboard Man turned around and headed for the blue door at the end of the hall—the odd man was walking with his arms raised in the air.

The students took off their headsets and followed. Rip and Mei were last to join the line, both refusing to make eye contact with each other.

They all left the INREAL GAMES studio and headed toward the school bus. Clipboard Man was handing the winners their BETA kits, which looked like small silver suitcases. And, as promised, each student got a piece of fat-free turnip cake.

Rip and Mei each took their piece and got on the bus, heads hanging low. Mei saw Sam, the boy who fell through the trapdoor, sitting at the back of the bus with his arms folded.

At least Rip and Mei had both had a chance; Sam spent the entire day waiting to go home.

As the bus pulled away from INREAL GAMES, Rip and Mei sat quietly next to each other taking bites of their turnip cake. Rip didn't think it was his fault they lost, but he was still feeling bad about ruining their chances.

He turned to Mei and said, "This is the most disgusting cake that has ever existed in all of time and space."

Mei nodded, but they kept eating it anyway.

VIRTUAL UNREALITY

The following week at school, the class was abuzz with the excitement from their field trip to INREAL GAMES. Angela was insufferable, boasting about coming in first and being chosen to play "some new video game." It was obvious she didn't even care about games that much—and yet, she was one of the BETA testers.

Mei was seated by the window in her classroom, waiting for the bell to ring. She couldn't wait to get home and just zone out in front of the TV. She hadn't played a game all week, not since the disastrous day at INREAL. She wished she could just erase the whole experience—pretend that it had never even happened. If only she hadn't been so focused on beating Rip!

At last the bell rang and there was an immediate cacophony of bustling and chatter as students made a break for the door. Mei began shoving her belongings into her schoolbag.

"And remember to do page ninety-eight of your textbook for homework!" Mrs. Berry, Mei's teacher, called out over the chaos. "I *will* be checking! Oh—Mei!" she exclaimed when she spotted her lagging behind. "I almost forgot."

Mrs. Berry handed her a folded note. Mei's brow furrowed. She opened the note. It read:

> Mei Lin Tam to come to the office after school please.

"I don't understand. Am I in trouble?" Mei asked.

Mrs. Berry shrugged. "I'm really not sure, Mei. Better head there right away." Seeing Mei's worried expression, she smiled reassuringly. "I'm sure it's nothing serious. Off you go!"

Mei shoved the note into her pocket and made her way quickly to the school's reception office. Taking a deep breath, she pushed the glass door open and was surprised to see Ripley standing there. He looked at her and held up a note, questioningly. Mei nodded, holding up her own note. What could this be about?

The office receptionist finished her phone call. "Ah, *you two*," she said, pointedly. "I have a package for you both." She lifted a large box wrapped in brown paper onto the desk. It did indeed have both their names on it.

Rip and Mei exchanged confused glances.

"Well . . . who's it from?" Rip inquired.

The receptionist pursed her lips and put on a pair of small spectacles that had been hanging around her neck on a beaded chain. She peered at the label. "It says INREAL GAMES—TOP SECRET." Her eyebrows raised.

Mei's heart skipped a beat. *What on earth?*

"Uh, OK—thanks!" Rip said quickly, snatching the box with both hands and heading for the door.

"Wait!" Mei hissed. "We don't know what it is! What if they sent it to us by mistake?"

She hurried out the door after him as he raced down the front steps of the school to the bus stop.

"Are you kidding me?!" Rip exclaimed. "It's from INREAL GAMES! Whatever it is, it's going to be *awesome*. So *what* if it's a mistake! I want to see what's inside. Don't you?"

Mei hesitated. It was very mysterious. Truthfully, the anticipation was driving her crazy. But she and Rip had failed so badly at the gaming contest. Why were *they* being sent something?

Before she could finish the thought, the bus arrived and Rip was already climbing on board.

"Well, hey—wait! It's addressed to me too. You can't just take it home!" Mei called after him.

Rip paused in the doorway, growing impatient. "So . . . come over to my house, then. We can't open it here on the bus where everyone will see. It says TOP SECRET." He held up the box to show her.

Mei frowned. "OK . . . well, I'll have to check with my mom first."

"Fine." Rip shrugged and he hurried to find a seat.

Mei followed him, keeping her eyes on the package. There was something *very strange* about all this.

Ripley dumped his schoolbag by the front door and headed toward the staircase. "My room's this way," he said, motioning for Mei to follow.

Mei hovered by the doorway for a moment before slipping her shoes off and setting them down by the door. "Shouldn't I say hi to your mom or something?" she offered.

"Rip? Is that you?"

A woman who Mei assumed was Rip's mother appeared in the hall. She was tall and had dark hair like Rip. She noticed Mei and welcomed her with a big smile. "Oh, hello there! Rip, I didn't know you were bringing a friend home!"

Mei blushed. "Hello, Mrs. Anders. I'm sorry—it was a kind of last-minute thing."

Mrs. Anders clasped her hands together excitedly. "No, I'm *thrilled,* truly! I think it's just wonderful. Rip doesn't really bring many friends over . . ."

This time it was Ripley's turn to blush. "Her name is Mei, Mom. And she's not even my friend, really. Well, I mean . . . we're in the same class at school. And . . . we . . ." Rip trailed off.

Mei stared at the floor, wishing it would swallow her whole.

Mrs. Anders laughed. "Fine. Well, I will leave you two 'non-friends' to have fun. Do you want some snacks? I'll bring some up. Oh, and I do like this—blue! How interesting!" She admired Mei's hair for a moment before making her way into the kitchen.

Mei's eyes widened at Rip, not sure what to say.

She could see Rip was trying to hide his embarrassment too. "Just . . . follow me," he said to Mei, heading upstairs.

Ripley's bedroom was very messy. Clothes were in disorganized piles all over the floor, with various old consoles, controllers, and cables buried beneath them. Posters of galaxies and nebulae taken by the Hubble telescope brightened the walls, and a precarious stack of gaming magazines was piled high in the corner.

"I like your consoles," Mei said, peering at what looked like an old CyberSystem from 1992.

Rip suddenly grinned, unable to hide his love for his collection.  "Thanks. My parents bought me a current-gen console for Christmas a few years ago, but I saved up for all the retro consoles on my own. I had to work a paper route and walk Mrs. Davidson's dog for eight months to afford the CyberSystem! But it's a seriously killer machine."

"I'll bet." Mei smiled back at him. "I have an original GameGo from, like, the '80s. I'm kind of a collector of portable devices."

"Nice!" Rip nodded, clearly impressed.

Mei thought he was becoming less annoying by the minute. They actually had quite a lot in common.

"Well . . . shall we see what's in the mysterious package?" Mei plonked herself down on the carpet, in one of the few spaces not covered in clothes.

"Definitely," Rip agreed, tearing the box open. "Are you ready?" He looked at her, suddenly very solemn.

Mei nodded. They both peered inside the box with a mixture of excitement and anticipation.

Fluffy white foam packing balls filled the box. Peeking through was a pair of what looked like very large ski goggles. Rip lifted the goggles out to examine, picking off any remaining foam balls that still clung to the head strap.

Mei noticed a second pair in the box and retrieved it. There was one for each of them.

"Is this . . . what I think it is?" Mei murmured.

Rip swallowed, turning the goggles over, feeling the weight of them.

"I think so," he replied. "A virtual reality device."

They sat in silence for a moment. The last time either of them had seen a virtual reality device, it was just a picture in a retro gaming magazine from the early '90s.

"I thought they stopped trying to make these." Mei's eyes were wide with wonder.

"Well . . . they were always kind of . . . flops. This is the first time INREAL GAMES has had this kind of tech. It could be a game changer, Mei!" Rip said. "There must be some kind of console with it. And a game."

Mei dug around inside the box. "I've got something!"

Her fingers closed over something round and smooth. It was a shiny black sphere, with a little

stand to set it on, and a power cord. Mei plugged
the cord in and set the sphere on its stand. They
both stared at it.

"I guess the game is already loaded in there,"
Rip observed.

The sphere shimmered and began to change
color—first pink, then yellow, then a solid red.
They waited. Nothing else happened.

"So . . . should we do this?" Mei picked up her
VR headset.

Rip nodded enthusiastically. "Absolutely!"

He pulled his own device over his eyes. Mei
pulled her headset on as well, and everything
plunged into darkness.

"Wait—" Mei said, suddenly. "We still don't
know why we were sent this! We lost,
remember?"

But the game had already started.

LOADING...

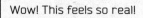

Wow! This feels so real!

Mei, this is AWESOME! I can see my hands and body and everything! And there's no controllers!

You LOOK so real. How is the game doing this?

It's only a loading screen—but it's amazing! True virtual reality!

I'm feeling cold. I'm actually FEELING cold!

Whoooooooooooahhhhh! Here we go!

Without warning, the floor disappeared beneath them and they started falling.

The falling sensation was incredible. Below, a colorful dot slowly came into view. The sky around them changed from white to faint blue.

They were really picking up speed now. Both of their mouths were catching the wind, making their faces puff out and fill up with air, showing their teeth. It was a pretty funny look. Rip stuck out his tongue at Mei.

"Rip, can you hear me?"

she shouted, trying to speak over the wind howling in their ears.

"Yes! This is amazing!" he said, as he did a somersault. Mei was steadying herself, arms outstretched like she'd seen skydivers do on TV. "LOOK!" Rip yelled, pointing far off into the distance. The ground was much closer now and toward the horizon they could see what appeared to be an erupting volcano.

Below them, a massive island full of green forests started to appear, surrounded by water. It was an ocean, and they were heading right for it.

It dawned on Rip and Mei that they did not appear to have a way to slow down. Rip began flapping his arms, still smiling. Mei was trying to see if there was some sort of menu she could activate by tapping her head, trying to find buttons on the VR headset. It was so strange, it didn't even feel like she was wearing it anymore.

"I can't find an inventory menu or anything!" she yelled.

"I don't think there is one!" Rip yelled back. "There's not even a health bar or any objective markers. I love it! So immersive!"

Rip was curious about what would happen when they hit the ground at this speed. Would they explode into bits? Would they bounce back up?

The ocean was right below them now; they'd hit it within minutes. Maybe they'd

just sink down into
some incredible
underwater zone!
Underwater levels were
usually terrible and not fun at all.
But if it felt this real, who cares!
Then Rip noticed something on Mei's
back. "You have a backpack!"

Mei reached behind and felt the backpack
and found a long cord. "You do too!" she
yelled at Rip.

Before she could say anything else, Rip
pulled the cord on his own backpack and
disappeared from her sight, flying high into
the air above her. She pulled her cord too,
and a parachute flew out of the pack, pulling
sharply at her shoulders as it caught the air.

They glided down gently, searching for a
safe place to land. In the distance they saw
a beach, and they both angled toward it.

"Watch out! Crabs!!" Rip called out as they
adjusted their trajectory.

CRABS! There were ALWAYS crabs in video games, and they were always really tough, with high armor ratings. Mei wasn't sure, but from this distance, it looked like the crabs were all wearing little hats.

Mei shouted back, "Let's not make them angry; we don't have any weapons!"

Suddenly, without any warning, their parachutes detached, sending Rip and Mei

plummeting toward the beach. They both screamed, and the crabs instantly turned toward them, raising their pincers high in the air and snapping them together. It looked like

they were dancing. Rip figured they had about thirty seconds before they hit the beach.

"What do we do?" Mei yelled. "I can't slow down or change direction. We're going to hit them! AND the beach! We'll be swarmed! What should we do?"

"We go FASTER!" Rip yelled back. He angled his body in a straight line and aimed for the middle of a large clump of the crabs. Mei smiled and did the same.

Sand, crabs, and little hats flew up into the air. Rip and Mei slowly stood up, a bit shaken, but also quite satisfied with their entrance. Strangely though, that landing kind of hurt!

Rip grabbed a handful of sand and held it up to the sun. The sky was blue now, the ocean was moving, the beach was long, and the sounds of seagulls filled the air.

"Mei, look at this sand! It's all cube-shaped!" he exclaimed. In fact, everything was cube-shaped. The sun, the waves, even the crabs, who were all now scampering away, dazed and upset. The whole world had a very square-like quality to it. "Retro!" he said.

Mei turned in circles, taking it all in. It wasn't an ugly-looking game. The square-shaped, blocky look to everything was a pretty common art style nowadays. But *this* VR technology was just so impressive. She walked backward and forward, trying to gauge if there was any lag or distortion. There was none. Nope! These controls were *perfect*.

"This really is amazing VR tech!" she said.

"I don't even feel sick!" Rip replied. Usually virtual reality games made him feel queasy within a few minutes. But this was different. He took a deep breath. "Hey! I can smell . . . I can actually smell the sea!"

Mei took a deep breath too. She smiled. "So can I! How does it do that?" She sniffed again, detecting a faint hint of seaweed.

They stood on the blocky beach, astounded at what they were experiencing. Rip and Mei had played a lot of video games. But they had never felt like they were actually *IN* one. Until now.

"So, what now?" Mei asked. Rip opened his mouth, about to speak, then closed it and pointed behind Mei. A robed figure hobbled along the beach toward them, waving a large wooden staff. They walked to meet him.

He wasn't blocky like the rest of the world. His character model was more realistic. There was still a slight pixelation to him, though. Not a huge amount, but he had just enough jagged and sharp edges for the two to notice. And, he was old. Really old. His hair was white as snow, and he had a tattered, messy beard. The staff he was carrying with him was a long, twisted tree branch, and at the very top they could see thin veins of red. It was an impressive staff, and Rip guessed it had fire properties of some sort, based on the look alone.

"Greetings!" the robed man said as he stomped his staff into the sand. "Welcome, to **DIG WORLD**! I am George the Wizard, and I will be your guide."

76

"George?" Mei said, looking at Rip. "That's not a very wizardy name."

"Totally. I'm going to call you ... Georgelboth of Crabberbay!" Rip said. "That's much more wizardy!"

Mei walked around George the Wizard. "How do we interact with him? I can't see any icons or dialogue choices or anything," she said. "Is it bugged?"

Rip reached out and touched the wizard's staff.

It felt solid!

"I don't know how they've done all this with just a VR headset. It must be doing something to our brain waves!" he said as he looked carefully at the old man's face. George was staring right at him. Rip put his hand around the staff. The old man didn't move.

"Don't do it, Rip!" Mei warned.

Rip looked at her, winked, and pulled at the staff.

There was a flash of light, a crack in the

air, and Rip flew
backward, leaving a trail
in the sand as his body
slid away from George
and Mei. George stood in
an attack stance for a
moment, and then
relaxed again, thumping his staff back into
the sand.

"OW!" Rip said, as he got up and dusted
square-shaped sand off his body. "That hurt."

Mei looked at Rip strangely for a moment.
"You're right! The beach landing hurt too.
Things hurt! Things *actually* hurt in this game!"

Rip giggled. "Virtual reality is awesome!"

Mei shook her head. They both stared at
George.

Mei cocked her head and said, "How do we talk to you?"

"With your voice, of course!" George replied.

"Whoa!" Rip exclaimed. "Voice recognition! Wow, this game has everything!"

"What do we have to do?" Mei asked George.

George paced back and forth, gesturing theatrically. "There are many things you can do in **DIG WORLD**. But, I'm not allowed to spoil it for you; there are rules even I have to obey. Part of the game is discovering what it is you need to do!" George's eye twitched a little as he said this. He was certainly a kooky character. He continued on. "I can tell you this—**DIG WORLD** is a very difficult game. You must survive for three days. You'll need to keep track of your vitals to stay alive. Here!"

George pointed his staff at Mei and Rip and yelled, "BACKSLASH SPAWN WRISTBAND ASSET FOUR!"

A flash of light erupted from the staff and

a wristband appeared on both Rip's and Mei's arms.

"I have replenished your health. That fall almost ended your journey before it began! You each now have three hearts. Manage your health carefully. This world ... it's not kind to new travelers ..." George seemed uneasy all of a sudden.

Rip looked up at the square-shaped sun, moving slowly across the sky. He turned back to George. "Um ... hi, George! Quick question. What happens when the sun goes down?" he asked.

George's eyes darkened. He looked a little scared. "Why ... the monsters come, of course."

And with that, he straightened up again, shook some sand off his robe, and walked away from the beach into the surrounding forest.

Mei and Rip turned to each other. It was time to get to work.

MINE OR DIE

The game world was more vast and wondrous than anything they had ever seen before. As they walked, Mei still couldn't believe how real everything felt. She could feel the wind on her skin. Hear it howling in her ears. The ground was firm beneath her feet.

Mei noticed a small flower with cubed yellow petals, and plucked it from the earth. Tiny cubes of dirt fell from its stem as she lifted it up to her nose and took a big whiff.

"Oh . . . ugh! POOH!" Mei exclaimed, dropping the flower instantly. "Flowers here smell like *farts* for some reason!"

Rip snickered. "Fart flowers!"

Mei rubbed her nose, trying to forget the smell. "Seriously, that was like rotten eggs or something."

Nevertheless, it was amazing that you could smell inside the game. She raised her hands up in front of her. Yes, they were still her own hands. She seemed to look the same, only . . . *digital.*

Rip scanned the horizon. "I don't see any monsters yet. What kind of game do you think this is?"

Mei felt a shiver of fear ripple through her at the thought of *actual monsters* in this world—likely to be as real as everything else appeared. She put the thought behind her, scooped up the stinky flower, and tucked it into her backpack. Rip looked at her with his eyebrows raised.

"Who knows; it could be useful," she said, looking around. "I don't see any

obvious objectives. It must be a survival game."

"Of course!" Rip snapped his fingers. "We'll need to build a shelter or something. Craft some tools—maybe harvest some materials…"

"Yes! We'll need wood to build a house. So…something to cut down trees. An axe?" Mei offered.

Rip nodded, excited to have a purpose. "I'm on it!" He jogged off toward the forest.

Mei looked around for a good place to build their safe house. The field she was standing in was definitely too open. They would need to find higher ground. Something protected by a good crop of trees, and with a high vantage point so they could see enemies coming. Mei smiled—already she felt her gamer experience coming in handy in this new digital environment. Game logic just came naturally to her.

The wind rustled through her dark hair.

Mei closed her eyes for a moment and breathed deeply. High in the sky, an orange cube-sun hung over the ocean, warming her face. Mei's eyes snapped open. The sun! If she and Rip didn't build their shelter by sundown—they could be swamped by monsters with nowhere to hide. A wave of panic crept over her, cold and terrifying. Everything in this game felt way more realistic than any other game she'd played before—and so did the threat of danger. She was suddenly very, very afraid.

Mei began to sprint in the direction Rip had gone.

Rip was admiring his handiwork—a pixelated axe crafted from a small stone he'd found and the branch of a cube-tree. To his amazement, by simply pressing one against the other, the two materials had fused together easily to

form the axe, shifting and morphing into the correct shape.

"Mei, check it out!" Rip said, waving the axe proudly as she approached. "An axe!"

"That's great!" Mei said, stopping to catch her breath. "I also found some fire stone. We're gonna need to build a fire."

Rip scoffed. "It's not even that cold!"

"No, not for warmth. For light. For when the darkness comes."

Rip's expression suddenly turned very serious, realizing what she meant. "And the monsters."

"Exactly. I wonder what they're like in this game."

Rip shuddered and turned to face the nearest tree. He began hacking at the trunk.

Mei dug around in her backpack and unloaded some more sticks, the fire stone, and some foliage. She wasn't sure what the exact materials were for creating fire in this world—in every game it was a different

formula. She tried leaves and fire stone first. Then fire stone and sticks. Then she tried leaves, fire stone, and sticks. A tiny spark appeared, then died out. "TIIIMMMMBBBEERRRR!" Rip cried out, and a cube-tree came tumbling to the ground. A cascade of wood blocks scattered near Mei.

"Hey—can I have one of those blocks of wood?"

"Sure!" Rip tossed a cube in Mei's direction. It was surprisingly light! It looked and felt like wood, but it was almost as if the physics of this world didn't obey the normal rules. She bounced the block easily between each hand.

Mei added the wood block to the foliage and sticks. As an afterthought she pulled out a few more stones she'd collected and added them to the pile. She tried the fire stone again. Sparks flew, and the pile of leaves,

wood, and stone shuddered slightly. Slowly, the items began to shift and move until they formed a neat little campfire, ringed in small stones. And finally—as if by magic—flames suddenly sprung to life and burned brightly.

"Nice one!" Rip cheered.

"Thanks." Mei beamed back at him.

This wasn't so hard, Mei thought, feeling more confident now she knew the formula.

"Hey." Rip tossed her a second axe he'd crafted. "Wanna help me chop more wood? We need to get this house up. *Fast*."

It was twilight. The cube-sun was sinking lower and lower down over the ocean in the distance, and the sky had turned from brilliant aqua to a deep blue.

Rip and Mei were exhausted. From piles and piles of wood in their forest sanctuary on the hill, they'd built themselves a modest but sturdy house. It had four walls, a roof, and two small windows—large enough to allow light in, but not so big that anything unwanted could climb through. There was an opening at the front of the house to get in and out. Mei had made wooden torches to set into the walls of the house for light.

It was starting to get darker.

"What else do we need?" Rip asked.

Mei shrugged. "I'm not sure. I don't think we have time to add anything fancy. We've got the basics, and that's what's important—"

THWACK!

An arrow hissed through the air and hit the side of the house just inches from where Mei was standing.

"Rip . . . it's starting."

"Hurry, get inside!"

Mei grabbed her backpack and ran with Rip inside the house. Rip turned around and reached for . . . nothing.

"We forgot to make A DOOR!" Rip cried.

THWACK!   THWACK!   THWACK!

Three more arrows came whizzing through the doorway and into their little sanctuary—which was no sanctuary at all if they couldn't keep the monsters out! Rip began wildly unloading blocks of wood from his backpack. A door. A door! Doors were made from wood, weren't they? What else would he need?

THWACK!

Rip felt a sharp bolt of pain in his back.

"RIP!!!" Mei screamed in alarm, reaching for him. But the arrow had vanished.

Rip grimaced, and the pain subsided. He looked down—half a heart had disappeared from his wristband. "I'm . . . OK. But we need to hurry. I'm on, like, two and a half hearts now."

A shadow passed over them both. Standing in the doorway was a dark figure, silhouetted against the light of the campfire outside. Mei swallowed, afraid to move. In the low light it appeared to be some kind of goblin, its skin tinged green. It let out a low, inhuman growl. They heard the creak of a bowstring. Rip was fumbling with the wood blocks, trying to arrange them on top of one another to create a door, afraid to turn around and face the fearsome creature.

Mei stood up, suddenly remembering her axe.

"Get OUT!" she yelled.

With every bit of strength she could muster, she hurled the axe at the creature—her aim sharp and true.

The axe hit its mark; the creature froze in place for a moment, its image appearing to shimmer slightly. All at once, it disintegrated into a pile of colored pixel cubes on the doorstep, which dissolved into nothing.

Mei stood, staring in disbelief, her chest heaving, hands shaking with adrenaline.

Rip held a neatly crafted door in his hands, and hurriedly shoved it into the doorway where it settled with a click. He turned to look at Mei. They stared at each other in silence for a moment.

Rip managed a wry smile.

"Mei . . . that was amazing. You are amazing."

But Mei's face remained somber.

"Rip . . ." she said slowly, her hands still shaking. "What do you think happens when these hearts on our wristbands are all gone?"

REINFORCEMENTS

T he goblin fight had been unexpectedly tough. A few hours had passed and Rip and Mei were both still a little shaken. Distant howls and cries of monsters had filled the air at times, but none had come bashing on the wooden door of their tiny square house.

Rip was at the window, staring into the night. He'd been on high alert since the attack. "I've fought a LOT of goblins in games before. But I've never had a fight like that," he said, still scanning the horizon for movement. He then relaxed as the sky started to lighten. "Not that I was scared or anything." Rip turned to Mei. "Just, you know ... it was intense."

"I know what you mean," Mei said, looking up from the floor where her backpack was

open and the inventory was spread out. There were a handful of wood cubes, a few stones, and some vines. They both knew it wasn't enough to build anything useful.

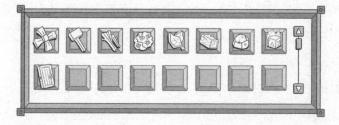

Rip moved from the window, satisfied they were safe for now, and sat down in front of Mei.

"I wonder how weird we look to my mom right now. You know, in my room with all this VR gear on," he said. "I bet we look quite silly, waving our arms about and jumping up and down."

Mei thought for a moment and said, "Oh no! What if she's taking photos of us and posting them online!" Rip raised his eyebrows and Mei's face dropped. "She wouldn't, would she?"

"Of course not." He smiled.

They both giggled and relaxed a little more.

Being connected to a completely different world for so long was starting to feel strange. They were both thinking about **DIG WORLD** less like a game and more like real life. Neither of them was ready to admit it out loud.

"Seriously though, I want to see this game through," Rip said. "I can't be called a NOOB, Mei! Ever! We have to beat this game!"

"Well I'm sorry to disappoint you, Rip, but we were already total NOOBS last night. We should've been more prepared," Mei said. "I think we can get through this if we just focus. We need to come up with a plan."

She started to pick up her materials and slide them into her backpack. As each block touched the pack, it disappeared into it, like magic.

"Agreed," Rip said, nodding. "We need

more materials. Stronger materials. And better weapons."

"Oh, we also need more space and a panic room."

"Good idea! Then we can retreat if things get out of hand again," Rip said.

"And we should stock up on some food," Mei noted, looking at her wristband. "We need to replenish our health—I've lost half a heart."

"Me too. I'm down to two."

A column of light shone through the window. Rip opened the door, and they cautiously stepped out into the dawn. The square sun rose over the horizon.

"Hope we'll be safe until nightfall," Rip said. "We have a lot of work to do today. Let's get digging!"

Rip and Mei grabbed their backpacks and headed into the forest.

"I've made an iron pickaxe!" Rip said, holding up a shiny pickaxe. He immediately started hammering away at a nearby rock. Cubes and cubes of different colored rocks flew out. It was much more efficient than collecting stone, and the tougher grades of rock might make for stronger craftables.

"Excellent." Mei grinned.

They were deep in the forest now. Huge, blocky trees rose up

around them, and there were plenty of giant rocks that looked like they'd been placed there on purpose. Mei looked up and saw the sun was just about above them. "Nearly midday," she yelled to Rip.

Mei had spent the morning harvesting more wood, and between the two of them they'd made excellent progress. They'd built a crafting table first, which allowed them to fuse more complex combinations of materials together. Now they had plenty of reinforced wooden planks, a stone door, enough torches to see them through the night, and more.

Mei arranged some cubes of wood and stone that Rip had fished out of the rocks into the outline of an axe and waited for the objects to fuse together. "What's missing?" she wondered. "Vines!"

Mei spotted some bushes nearby. She went over and pulled and pulled until she had a decent bunch of straight, cubeish vines. When Mei added them to the axe

shape on the table, they fused together instantly and made an axe with a dark-brown wooden shaft and a sharp black top. It looked even stronger than Rip's! "This will do nicely!"

She made another one for Rip and placed them in her bag, along with the remaining materials.

"OK, I think I have enough stone and iron to reinforce the house," Rip said, throwing his own bag over his shoulder. "Let's get back."

The door was open.

"Did you leave the door open?" Mei asked Rip.

"No, did you?" he replied.

"Of course not! I would never leave the door open."

"Well neither would I!" Rip said. "Someone has been inside. They might *still* be inside. Let's be careful."

"Catch!" Mei said, as she pulled out the new axes and threw one to Rip. They approached stealthily along the tree line, trying not to be spotted.

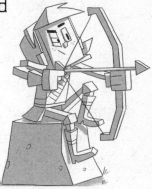

"Your house is boring," said a voice behind them. "You don't even have a pool." Rip and Mei spun around, axes raised to the ready.

"Angela?!" Rip shouted. *What was she doing here?* She was covered in heavy leather armor and had a bow and arrow drawn, pointed right at them.

"A pool is a pointless addition to a survival house," Mei said, lowering her axe. Rip didn't lower his.

"Lower your weapon, Ripley. I'm in full heavy armor, and I have iron-tipped arrowheads. You won't even get close." Angela snickered. "Where's your armor?"

Rip looked embarrassed. He hadn't even thought to craft protective gear! All he could think about was reinforcing the house.

"I don't want armor," he lied. "It would just slow me down."

Mei lowered Rip's axe. "Angela, we're not your enemy; we're trying to survive the night. Just like you," she said.

Angela let go of an arrow and it whizzed past, inches away from Rip's head. It hit their house and knocked a few blocks out of the wall, exposing the interior.

"Ugh!" Rip growled. "Leave our house alone!"

"Ooooo," Angela said mockingly, "sharing a house are we? Are you married now?"

"WE'RE NOT MARRIED!" Mei yelled, a little too loudly.

"With a tiny house like that, good luck. My place is massive. See!" Angela pointed off into the distance.

Even from here, Rip and Mei could make out a massive wooden castle-like structure. "I've built an entire castle. I've even got a moat," she gloated.

"Did you make the whole thing out of just wood?" Mei asked.

"Yep, isn't it awesome?" Angela replied. "It's the biggest castle I've seen so far. And I can see everything from the top."

Rip looked at Angela. "Is it really ALL made of wood? Haven't you reinforced any—" Rip stopped himself. Then he said casually, "Wow. That sounds like a great castle, Angela."

"Yep, it's pretty neat. Lots of big spaces to kick back and sit these three days out," Angela said. "Well, this conversation is as boring as your house. I have much better things to do. Later, losers!" Angela swung her bow over her shoulder and disappeared back into the forest.

Rip turned to Mei. "That castle isn't going to hold. Wood is great

when you're starting out, as a base. But big creatures, or anything that explodes, are going to tear a hole right through it."

Mei nodded.

"OK. Let's get to building," she said. "I've been thinking some more about the layout. We need lots of rooms. A room for some beds, a main living room for weapons and to keep watch, and a treasure room for our spare materials."

"That sounds perfect," Rip replied. "I'll reinforce the safety room with double stone and make some stone doors as well. And we should add a second layer to every other wall in the house. That'll be one more layer enemies would have to bash through."

Mei nodded. "Plus, if we get an explosive breach, it's less likely to be catastrophic. Let's do this!"

The sun was just slipping to the edge of the
horizon as Rip and Mei placed their last blocks.
Their four-room house was now a tough little
fortress. The living room had a stone door
and a variety of axes and spears at the ready.

"It just looks so boring," Rip said.

"Rip, when it comes to house construction,
looks aren't everything," Mei said.

It was a good, functional, and practical
structure for a variety of situations, which
was all that mattered right now.

"I've got it!" Rip said. "I'll be right back!"

"Rip! The sun is about to go down!" Mei yelled
after him as he ran off toward the beach.

Mei went inside and triple-checked the
walls and weapons. Everything was set. They
were secure.

"OK! Come outside!" Rip called out.

Mei stepped outside to find that Rip had
built a low wall around the front of their
house. And within it was a small army of

around twenty crabs, who were all wearing tiny top hats.

Rip was riding the biggest one, which had a mustache and a monocle.

"Meet Sir Crabbington of Beachburry and his army of crab minions!" Rip said. "Turns out crabs really like berries." He threw a handful of berries to Sir Crabbington's minions, who frantically scrambled around, fighting over them. "I think we've agreed that they won't attack us as long as we give them berries. And maybe they'll defend our place during the night. I'm not entirely sure, as they only seem to communicate with clicks and gestures."

Mei smiled. "Now that is brilliant!"

Ripley and Mei pulled their stone door closed just as the square sun went down for a second time, to the sounds of top-hat-wearing crabs clicking their claws and eating berries.

NIGHT TERRORS

Rip and Mei built a small stone fireplace at the rear of the house so that they could keep warm and cook food. Not eating anything but berries had started to make them feel weak and tired.

Mei tapped her wristband nervously. "How did I end up on two hearts?!"

Rip looked grim. "I'm on one and a half. We need to eat more."

"If we roast the vegetables we collected over the fire, I bet we'll get more health out of them," Mei said cheerily, happy to be safe inside their stone fortress.

"Awesome," Rip replied. "I was getting a little tired of berries!"

Mei placed six pixelated carrots and a large, blocky turnip onto the fire and waited.

The fire was a collection of orange, red, and yellow cubes that danced around one another, giving off a strange, artificial glow. It certainly didn't crackle and pop like a regular fire, and the heat that came from it felt strange—it reached their bodies without actually making them feel any warmer. But they were glad for the cheery atmosphere it provided.

Rip toyed with his wristband. He looked at Mei and was suddenly very glad to have such a strong gamer as his companion in this

crazy virtual world. Going it alone would have been tough.

"I wonder how Angela is doing," Rip said, a wry smile creeping across his face.

Mei glanced over to him. "She seemed pretty confident. And that castle was impressive—even if it isn't made out of the strongest materials. Do you . . . think she's alone in there?"

Rip thought for a moment. "I doubt it. Her fancy castle is probably a rush job, not strong enough to withstand the monsters. I can't believe she almost *shot* me!"

Mei snorted, "I can. She's awful." Then she added, "I do hope she's OK, though."

Mei tossed Ripley a roasted carrot and started munching on one herself. The hearts blinked back to life on their wristbands.

Rip laughed. "So what if she isn't! It's just a game, Mei. I know that was crazy last night, with the goblins, but none of this can be real, remember?"

"I know ..." Mei's voice faltered. "It just ... it *felt* real, you know?"

They were both quiet for a moment. The carrots tasted like something that perhaps had once been carrots, but had forgotten what a carrot was supposed to taste like. As the faint flavor hit their mouths, it disappeared instantly.

"Rip?" Mei served them both another carrot, saddened by how unsatisfying the vegetables were as a meal. "Why do you think we were sent the game? Only the winners of the gaming competition at INREAL were supposed to get access to the BETA. So ... why did we get it? It doesn't make sense."

Rip's eyes were fixed on the fire. "I don't know," he said thoughtfully. "Could have been a mistake. Like a clerical error or something." He didn't sound convinced.

"I doubt INREAL make mistakes when it comes to unreleased games," Mei said. "They're pretty intense with their security. All the winners had to sign those crazy legal forms before they left the studio."

Rip didn't reply. He'd been so excited to play the game, he hadn't questioned receiving it and simply put it down to a stroke of good luck. It definitely *was* strange—why hadn't he and Mei had to sign anything before they could take the package?

"We should get some rest," Rip said softly, not wanting to think about it anymore. The idea that they were mixed up in something wrong, or that they might have made a mistake in choosing to play this game, gave him a sick feeling in his stomach.

Outside, they could hear the distant growl of an unknown monster.

"Rip. RIP! Wake UP!"

Rip felt panicked arms shaking him, and he scrambled to his feet. "What is it? More goblins?!"

"Look," Mei was standing with her face pressed against the window. "Angela's castle. It's on *fire*!"

Rip raced to the window and looked out too. Sure enough, the wooden structure was covered in digital flames, which flickered brightly in the darkness of the early morning.

"Can you see Angela anywhere?"

Mei shook her head anxiously. "What should we do?"

Rip looked at her. "What do you mean?"

"Well . . . we should help her, shouldn't we?"

"Why would we? She was mean to us, remember? The arrow? My *head*? Besides . . ." Rip scrambled for words. "She . . . she's always such a know-it-all and

thinks she's so much better than everyone else. But she's *not* a good gamer, Mei. This is just proof of that. She probably set fire to the castle herself by mistake!"

Mei frowned. "I just ... we still don't really know how everything works here. I think we should check and see if she's OK."

Rip felt a wave of guilt creep over him and sighed. "Maybe ... maybe you're right." He turned back to the window and studied the blaze. Angela was annoying. And they had used all their skills and knowledge of survival games to get this far. Why should they risk everything just to help *her*?

But there was still an uneasy feeling in the pit of his stomach that told Ripley that something wasn't quite right. And it wasn't going away.

ROOOAAARRR!

"WHOA!" Rip stumbled backward, hitting the floor with a thud.

His vision had suddenly been obscured by an enormous snarling head—it was some kind of tiger-like creature, covered in flames.

"Oh my gosh. What *is* that?" Mei screeched.

"I d-don't know," Rip stammered, "but it looks like there are more of them."

Mei backed against the wall farthest from the window. "It . . . can't get *in* here, can it?"

The creature scratched angrily at the window—terrifying yellow, pixelated eyes fixed on them both. They could hear growling sounds all around the perimeter of the house. Who knows how many tiger creatures were out there? But it seemed they were surrounded.

"I think we're safe," Rip said, reaching for his axe just in case.

The creature snarled but moved from the window and began scratching at their front door. Rip braced himself and made his way to the window that overlooked where Sir Crabbington of Beachburry and his minion army were. Rip poked his head up just high enough to peer out, but he couldn't see anything except a gap in the stone wall that had surrounded the house. "Oh no," he whispered, "they're gone."

"I'm sure they're OK," said Mei. "They're

probably safer than we are right now!" She
looked out toward Angela's castle again. The
fire had stopped. All she could see now was
gray, cube-columns of smoke. "I seriously
hope these tiger-things aren't over where
Angela is. Because it looks like she doesn't
have a shelter right now."

"Well, we can't go out now. We'd never
make it through the forest," Rip said.

Mei nodded reluctantly in agreement.
"Maybe . . . she built a safe room," she offered,
hopefully. "You know, for her gear. In case she
gets raided. She could be taking refuge in that."

Rip shrugged. "Not many people know to build
those. I guess we'll find out in the morning."

The roar of the flaming tiger continued at
their door. Mei looked down at her wristband
and again began wondering what would
happen when all the little health hearts had
disappeared. *What would an in-game death
feel like? Would it hurt?* Mei shivered,
realizing the thought genuinely scared her.

LOOT 'N' SCOOT

Mei was first out the door at the break of day. Her backpack was full of food, materials, and all the tools and weapons they had. If Angela had made it through the night, Mei wanted to make sure she had enough materials to help her rebuild.

"Hold up!" shouted Rip as he shut the door, trailing after Mei, who had started jogging toward Angela's wrecked castle. "There's no need to rush, the monsters are gone."

"I just want to make sure she's OK," Mei said, not breaking her stride.

Rip chased after her. "Mei, there's only one day to go. I don't want to lose because of Angela. It'll be nighttime before we know it. We have more important things to do! We

could use some more food, and I'd like to build
a second story on the house for a lookout.
Also, we need protective gear . . ."

Mei stopped, almost bumping into Rip. "Rip.
You can go do all that if you want. But I'm
just going to go over there, say hello, and
check to see if Angela's OK. OK?"

"Waste of time," Ripley said.

Mei glared at him.

Rip gave in. "Fine. But I'm not talking to her."

They turned around and started jogging
again toward the ruined wooden castle in
the distance.

There wasn't much left. What hadn't burnt
away into ash blocks was pretty damaged.
Rip and Mei were staring at what they
thought was the entrance of the castle.

"That's where they got in," Rip said quietly,
pointing to a gaping hole on the right side of
the structure. "You can see the scatter

patterns. Something exploded. That's a big breach."

These games always had creatures that blew up, and they were especially devastating when you had weak or thin walls.

Mei walked forward, kicking blocks of dirt and ash aside as she went.

"ANGELAAAAAA!"

There was no answer. Rip and Mei headed deeper into the ruined castle, past a huge rectangular hole, which they realized was probably the remains of Angela's swimming pool. It still had a little bit of water in it.

ANGELAAAAA!

"I hate to say it, but this pool actually looks pretty good," said Rip, kicking a cube of dirt into the pool water. It bobbed a little, then sank to the bottom.

Mei said nothing and continued to look around.

Rip continued. "There's no way she survived this. It's a full-scale breach. If she wasn't taken out by the explosion then she'd have been overwhelmed by the monsters for sure."

Rip could tell Mei was taking this all very seriously.

"Mei, chill out already! It's just a game," Rip said, trying to reassure her. "Angela's probably back in her house in the real world throwing a mega tantrum."

Mei was ignoring Rip. Ripley hated being ignored. It just made him want to get her attention even more.

"I'm going upstairs," he said in a huff and headed up a broken flight of stairs to the second level.

Mei walked to the back of the castle. Very little was distinguishable, but she found an open door that led outside. "Maybe you got out after all..."

Then Mei saw a backpack lying on the ground, next to a wristband. Mei tugged at her own and it wouldn't budge. Her heart sank. Sure enough, she looked at the discarded wristband's display:

ANGELA CARSON—GAME OVER. DE-SPAWNED BY ENRAGED FLAMETIGER. END OF LINE.

Rip was standing in front of a silver chest. He bent down and lifted the lid. He was surprised to find it wasn't locked. He peered inside. "OH MY!" he said, pulling out a silver bow, with forty stacks of silver arrows. "Jackpot!"

Rip always played ranged classes when he could. He loved lining up shots, and the sound the arrows made as they flew through the air. He slung the bow over his shoulder and put the arrows in his bag.

"What else have we got here . . ."

"Mei! Mei! Look at this!" Rip trundled out of the castle's back door toward Mei. He was dressed in full, heavy leather gear, with a large knight's helmet, complete with a faceguard. "I know it doesn't go together, but I just love faceguards." Rip lifted the guard up and down, pretending it was his mouth, and said, "Excuse me, fair maiden, can thou point me to the eating house?"

"Angela's gone. I found her bag and her wristband." Mei held them toward Rip, who raised his faceguard up to a resting position. "Look at this.

Her wristband says 'de-spawned by a flametiger.' What does de-spawn mean?" Mei asked.

"I don't know, but it can't be good. I knew her castle wouldn't survive the night in that state! Angela should have spent less time in the pool and more time learning how to build!" Rip said. "What a survival **NOOB**."

"She's gone, Rip! Don't you care? She doesn't exist anymore!" Mei shouted.

"Whoa! Mei! Calm down!" Rip said, taking a step backward. "Come on, it's just a GAME!"

Mei sat down on the ground. "You're ... you're right." She put her head in her hands and sighed. "Then why doesn't it feel like one, Rip?"

"Because it's really *good*!" he said. "Check out this sweet bow!"

Rip shot an arrow straight up into the air. It disappeared into the sky.

"I think I just need a quick break," Mei said. "I'm logging off for a bit, I feel a little sick."

Mei put her hands to her head to feel for the VR helmet and take it off.

"Whoa, whoa, whoa ..." Rip said. "If you leave now you might not be able to get back in! We only have one night left to survive. Then we win!"

"I'm telling you, Rip, this feels too weird. I'm sure I'll be able to log back in." Mei was still struggling to take off the headset. "Rip, I can't seem to take it off."

"Fine. Here, I'll help." Rip put his hands on Mei's head, where the headset should be. But all he could feel was her hair. "Um ... I can't feel it. Hang on." Rip grabbed a clump of Mei's hair and started pulling.

"OW! Stop that!" Mei shouted.

"Almost got it!" Rip kept pulling.

"Ow! Ow! I mean it, Rip! Stop!" Mei said and pushed Rip

so hard he fell down. "I don't understand. Why can't I take it off?"

Rip moved his hands up and tried to feel his own headset. "I can't feel mine either."

They stared into each other's eyes, suddenly very worried. Mei looked at Angela's wristband and then up at the sky. The sun felt warm on her face. There was a breeze, full of the scent of ash and wood from Angela's castle.

"It's real," Mei said.

"What's real?" Rip asked.

"I don't know why we didn't work this out earlier. This isn't a game, Ripley. It's real," Mei said.

"That's nonsense," Rip said. "It . . . it can't be. This is all just video-game code. It's just lines of 0s and 1s that draw and populate a video-game world. It's just gotten into our brain and paralyzed us somehow!"

"Then why can't we leave?" Mei asked. "Why can't we feel our VR headsets? Why

hasn't your mom come in the room to talk to us? Think about it, Rip! We've been playing this game for two days. Two actual days." Mei was starting to look a little panicked. "We haven't even gone to the bathroom! Why don't I need to pee, Rip? That's really weird!

WHY DON'T I NEED TO PEE?!"

There was an awkward silence. Rip looked at Mei, who was slightly embarrassed.

PFFFFFFFFFFFFFFT! Rip farted.

"You can still fart," he said.

"That's gross." Mei stifled a giggle. "And SO not important right now!"

She took a step back, her expression turning serious again. Mei was putting the pieces together. The strange Clipboard Man. The empty desks. The unusual VR gear. How they could run about without bumping into the walls of Rip's bedroom. Something wasn't

right about this game, and Mei was starting to get scared.

"It's ... it's just great technology!" Rip said, not really believing what he was saying. He started patting down his body trying to find some sort of switch or way to unplug. "We're being tricked! In our brains! This isn't REAL! We're not actually HERE!"

"But what if we are?" said Mei.

There was a low rumbling, and then a long, deep, bellowing laugh filled their ears. It suddenly got very cold. Mei rubbed her arms and shivered. Then it started to get dark.

Rip and Mei stood up and looked to the sun. It was moving faster than before, sinking toward the horizon. Turning day into night. There was a howling off in the distance, and Rip and Mei could see red eyes bobbing up and down, getting closer and closer.

The ground next to them suddenly exploded

upward, showering Rip and Mei with dirt.
Little crabs with top hats came pouring out
of the hole, including Sir Crabbington of
Beachburry.

Standing with them was George the
Wizard.

ALL THAT GLITTERS

They grabbed their packs and sprinted. Well, *Mei* sprinted. The armor Rip had collected was sturdy and strong—but it was *heavy* too. He huffed and puffed under the weight of it, holding his bow tucked firmly under his arm.

Mei's eyes scanned their surroundings. She pointed. "There!"

Rip followed her gaze to a small, dark cave that sat nestled in a rocky cliff face. He nodded. "Let's go!"

When at last they reached the yawning mouth of the cave, the

terrifying calls of night monsters could be heard in the distance. This certainly wasn't the safest place they could be, but it would have to do for now. The sky turned a shimmering gold, and then midnight blue. Moonlight flooded from above.

Their sturdy stone house was too far away for them to get to in the dead of night.

Rip dropped his bow with a groan and put his hands on his knees, panting, trying to catch his breath. "What the . . . ? What is going on? Did you hear that laughing? Who was that?!"

"I don't know, I don't *know*!" Mei cried with growing panic. "The sun barely reached the midpoint, right? Why did it set so quickly? We didn't even get a full day!"

"This isn't *fair*! It's bugged or something," cried Rip, pulling the helmet off his head. "Now what?!"

Mei was hurriedly digging around inside her backpack—trying to muddle her way through the jumble of miniature items inside. "Should we try and build a wall or something? Barricade ourselves in?" she wondered. "Aha!"

Mei produced a large wooden torch, from which flames sprung to life when she removed it from the bag. She lifted the torch high, examining the roof, walls, and entrance of the cave. It was dull and dark, although it seemed as if large blocks of stone had been purposefully hacked from the walls.

"Wait a minute..." Mei studied the walls carefully. "This isn't a cave..."

"It's a *mine!*" Rip finished the sentence for her. "I wonder if this was Angela's."

"Should we check it out?"

Rip looked back over his shoulder, taking in the sight of the ruined castle, the smoke, the ominous night sky outside. Somewhere, a terrifying howl rang out.

"If we stay here, we're done for anyway." Rip pulled the helmet back onto his head and equipped his bow, his expression grim through the metal grill of his visor. "Let's keep going."

By the light of Mei's torch, they ventured forth into the blackness. The torchlight flickered across the ceiling, casting strange, dancing shadows as the tunnel began to slope gently downward.

"Rip," Mei spoke softly, her expression solemn. "Do you think ... Angela is ... dead? I mean ... I know the game said she had reached the end of the line ... but you don't think that means ... for real, do you?"

Rip shuddered, remembering the sight of her belongings just sitting there in a heap on the floor. "I...honestly don't know." He watched Mei's shoulders slump as she trudged on ahead of him, resigned. "Hey, listen to me." He spun her around to face him. "We're going to find a way out of this. We have to. This...whatever this is...it started as a game. There has to be a way out of it. If there's a bug or something that's stopping us from getting out—there'll be a way around it. Some kind of...'reset' button. For all we know, we could just be sitting in my room right now, and my mom is about to walk in any minute and take our headsets off and offer us that snack she promised!"

Mei perked up a little at the thought. "Do you really think so?"

Rip shrugged. "Sure!"

"Seems weird that she hasn't already. I guess time must move a lot faster here. Feels like we've been here for days. But that

can't be right..." Mei's dark eyes were thoughtful, distant. She turned to resume their descent into the mine. "Hey!" she said suddenly. "Look at this!"

Mei hurried down the sloped pathway to where one of the crumbled, blocky walls of the tunnel had been hollowed out into a little alcove. Cubes of stone in various sizes were stacked all over the floor. She lifted her torch and peered carefully into the recess of the rock wall. Something glittered.

Rip caught up behind her and squinted over her shoulder. "Is that... what I think it is?"

A smile spread across Mei's face. "You betcha. It's..."

"... *diamond*!" they both said at once.

Mei wedged the torch into a chink in the tunnel wall and pulled a sturdy pickaxe from her backpack.

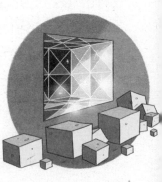

"Rip! Let's grab some. This stuff is invaluable when it comes to crafting!"

Rip nodded enthusiastically, slinging his bow over his shoulder and pulling out his own pickaxe. They both began chipping away at the rocky alcove, revealing block after block of glittering diamond. Pale, luminescent light shimmered across their faces as they lifted each precious cube from the mineshaft wall, carefully loading them into their packs.

After a while, the small alcove had grown into the beginnings of a separate tunnel. But the diamond, it seemed, was in limited supply, and no matter where they aimed their pickaxes, the mineshaft now only yielded stone.

Mei huffed with exertion. "I think that might be it," she said.

"Yeah," Rip agreed, "diamond is usually pretty rare in games like this. But we got a decent haul!"

They both grinned. It felt good to have something go their way at last. With this material they could make extremely powerful weapons and armor—maybe even items with magical properties!

"We should get going," Rip said, gathering his things.

Mei was pulling on her pickaxe. "Hey!" she grumbled, "my pick is stuck!"

"It doesn't matter. We can make you a shiny new one out of diamond! Let's just go."

"No!" Mei replied firmly. "We don't have enough to waste it on tools! We have to save it. Just help me with this, would you?"

Rip rolled his eyes. "Fiiiine."

They both took hold of the pickaxe handle and pulled with all their might. It seemed wedged in hard, but with their combined efforts, it came free at last. The pair tumbled backward as the pick fell from the wall, along with a cascade of stone blocks.

"Phew!" Mei panted, dusting herself off. "That was tough. And, hey—look at this!"

She held up a small disc of bronze metal. They both studied the object intently.

"What do you think it is?" Rip wondered, peering at the strange markings that were etched into one side of the treasure.

"The markings make it look like it's a piece of something larger. Like a small plate, maybe? Or a medallion?"

"Well that's probably important. When are medallions ever not important?!"

Mei laughed. "Well, we won't know what it is for sure until we find the rest of it. Should we keep looking for more pieces?"

Rip was no longer concerned with the medallion, however. His eyes were wide with panic as cubes of bright blue water began filling the hole behind Mei where the pickaxe had just been. Water blocks were flooding the tunnel at an alarming rate.

WEB OF WORRY

"**D**on't stop!" Mei yelled as she and Rip clambered and stumbled upward. The mine was crudely dug, and it was a challenge to not trip over stray squares and rough steps. "This mine is terrible!" Mei complained. "You never build in one direction like this! It floods too easily!"

"Obviously!" Rip said. "But perhaps now is not the time for analysis, Mei! Just keep moving!"

Rip did his best to keep up. His armor was slowing him down, but there was no time to take it off. The sound of raging water was deafening now.

Rip shot a glance behind them. Cubes and cubes of water were tumbling toward them,

swallowing up the mine below. The water was forming a sharp, jagged wave and it was not slowing down. Rip was scanning the walls for an exit, some way to escape the cube tsunami, but nothing revealed itself.

Mei was also trying to come up with a plan. They couldn't dig left or right—the water would find its way in and they'd drown. They couldn't dig down, it would fill up instantly and they would drown. They couldn't dig up, there was no time to start building. And even if they did, they might be trapped beneath hard materials they couldn't get through, or just run out of air before they could dig a way out.

It struck Mei that maybe in this world, she didn't even need air! But she couldn't exactly test that theory. For now, all she could do was keep climbing and running, and do her best not to drop her torch at the same time.

Then she saw it. A bright square in the

distance. It was the opening. They were going to make it.

Mei smiled and looked back at Ripley. "Rip, I can see the entrance! Come on!"

But Rip had stopped running. There was terror in his eyes. "No, we can't!" he said. "Look again!"

Mei turned. The light square was moving. It was coming toward them, fast. One square quickly turned into two. Then into twenty. The squares had eyes. They had teeth. They had legs. EIGHT legs. The bright squares were giant spiders, and they were also on fire!

"Rip! What do we do?" Mei cried.

"Look, shine the light here!" Rip shouted.

Mei waved the torch in Rip's direction, revealing a vein of yellow within a partially dug-out wall.

"Is that what I think it is?" Mei said.

"It's sulfur," Rip replied. "Give me the torch!"

Cubes of water were now bumping and dissolving into their legs from behind. The wave was almost upon them. The fire spiders were covering the mine walls in front of them—they'd reach the two of them in a matter of seconds. Mei threw the torch to Rip.

"Stand back!" Rip said.

"You'll blow up, Rip!" Mei yelled.

"It's OK!" Rip lowered his helmet's visor. "I'm geared for this!" He thrust the torch into a section of sulfur.

The vein lit up in a chain reaction along the wall, then violently exploded in a flash of white. Rocks and dirt flew out of the wall, obscuring Ripley completely.

The ground beneath Mei dissolved. Mei screamed as she fell through the cave floor in a shower of dirt and sand. She grabbed wildly for anything she could get a hold of, but she was in a cascade.

Mei fell for a few moments more and was suddenly halted in midair by what felt like a hammock. She covered her face as more cubes tumbled and crashed over her.

When the cascade was over, Mei opened her eyes. She was suspended in a web of strong, white sticky material.

Mei checked herself, pulling her arms from the sticky web with some difficulty. She was bruised, but nothing appeared to be broken.

She checked her health meter. She had lost a heart in the explosion but still had two left. Mei peered down through the white strands to see she wasn't that far from the ground. The cavern was warm and surprisingly well lit.

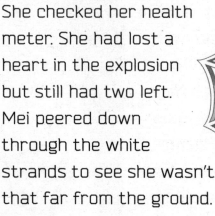

"OK, Mei. Let's think this through." She took off her backpack, which was still completely intact. She pulled out five vines and twisted them into one another. With a *sshhhuuk* sound, they formed a vine rope. Mei threw the rope over the side, and fastened her end to a thick-looking strand of the web hammock. She slowly pulled her legs and torso free, and clambered over the side to climb down.

Ripley blinked open his eyes. Everything was out of focus for a moment or two, but eventually shapes started to form in front of him. He couldn't move. His arms and legs felt stuck. He couldn't even turn his head. He realized he was trapped in something very sticky and very strong. He had a mammoth headache—it felt like he had eaten a giant scoop of ice cream too quickly. He started to panic a little.

Slowly, the reality of the situation began to sink in. The cave collapsing around them . . . the rushing water . . . the fire spiders.

This felt real. It *was* real.

The video-game world was real, and it was trying to kill them. He was worried about how many hearts would be left on his wristband—he really took a hit from that explosion.

Rip tried again to move, but it was hopeless. He coughed out tiny cubes of dirt and took a deep breath.

"MEI! MEI!"

The words echoed for a while, which led Rip to believe he was in a larger cave than before. Suddenly, a large, blocky body slid down toward him with four long, spiky legs expanded out on each side. Its torso started to glow red, which in turn lit up the creature's face.

To Ripley's amazement, the face was familiar.

Then, it spoke.

It was Angela. Angela was a spider. A BIG spider.

And she looked mad.

LITTLE MEAT. LITTLE THIEF.

NOT SO ITSY BITSY

Mei shuddered, tearing the long, sticky strands of spider's web from her arms and legs. This was a disaster. Where on earth was Ripley? She desperately hoped he was OK.

"RIIIIP?" she called out hopefully.

In the distance, she thought she heard someone yell.

"RIPLEYYY?" she called again, this time louder and more urgent. But there was only the dark, eerie silence of the cave.

Mei took a better look at her surroundings. This part of the cave glowed a glittering blue-green. Light seemed to be generated by tiny glow-worm-type creatures that covered the ceiling and walls. The light was so glowing, she didn't even need her torch.

Mei had to find Ripley and get out of here.

Around her, strands of silky web stuck to the glowing walls, and Mei could see they continued along the tunnel in one direction.

She didn't like the idea of heading the same way a spider might have gone, but it seemed to be sloping up toward the surface. Mei decided it was the best way to go. She adjusted the bag over her shoulders and followed a trail of silk into the turquoise oblivion.

A horrible feeling of dread filled Ripley's stomach as Spider-Angela began slowly, menacingly advancing. Seeing her face distorted into the shape of the spider was positively horrifying—it was Angela, and yet not Angela. She had been completely transformed into an inky-black pixelated arachnid. How had this happened?!

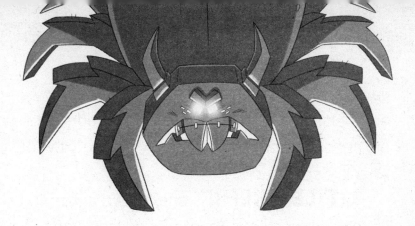

LITTLE THIEF. I WILL EAT.

Eat?!! Does she mean me?!

"A–Angela?" Rip swallowed nervously, struggling against the bonds of the spider's web. "Angela, it's me . . . Ripley. Angela, something has *happened* to you. Inside the

game. You've got to snap out of it! I can try
and help you!" Ripley was writhing madly in
his cocoon beneath the terrifying red glow of
Angela's spider-body.

"LITTLE THIEF!!!" she hissed again,
rearing up with her front spider legs, her
fangs snapping wildly as she prepared to
lunge at him.

Little thief. What was she talking about?

Spider-Angela lunged forward and sprayed
some sort of venom. A burst of burning liquid
splattered over him—it was searing hot, like
lava, and Ripley cried out in pain. But the
sticky strands that were binding him began to
loosen. He managed to wrestle one hand free,
at the same time noticing half a heart blinking
on his health meter before disappearing
entirely. He was down to one heart!

Little thief. Little thief.

It had to mean something! Rip had to think
quickly—he needed something, *anything*, that

would buy him some time. He couldn't access his bow, but he lifted his free hand to the helmet on his head.

The helmet. *Of course!* He had looted those items from Angela's castle! So she *did* remember something! Rip hastily pulled the helmet off and in one swift movement hurled it in Angela's direction.

It hit her square in the chest, sending her flipping over onto her back, her spider legs wiggling madly. Ripley wrenched himself free of the remaining web, most of which had now dissolved in the fire-venom.

For the moment, Spider-Angela seemed stuck, unable to flip herself back over. Rip scrambled over to her, holding his hands cautiously out in front of him.

CLUNK!

"Angela," Ripley said tentatively, "I know you're in there."

The spider's legs stopped wiggling.

"It's me. *Ripley*. Listen, we're . . . we're in a video game. Something has happened to you, and we all have to try and get out. There's . . . some kind of fault with the VR headsets or something. But as soon as we find a way to complete this level, everything will be OK!"

Angela turned her head and stared at him blankly with her large spider eyes. For a moment, it seemed as though she recognized him. She opened her mouth and closed it again. She seemed confused. Heartened, Rip continued.

"You can come with us and we'll find a way out together. And we can try and get you back to . . . normal."

"BACK. NORMAL." Angela shook her head as she tried to form a sentence. She seemed all muddled. **"CAN'T. ESCAPE. BIG LAVA . . ."**

Rip frowned. "What's Big Lava?"

Angela's eyes grew larger and wider. **"BIG LAVA. MADE ME LIKE THIS. CONTROLS EVERYTHING. NO ESCAPE."** She struggled to get the words out.

Rip could hear the fear in her voice. He suddenly felt very cold all over. "Angela, I don't . . . I don't understand. What do you—"

A thunderous rumble shook the cave. The room began to shudder, rocks and dirt crumbling down from the ceiling. The jolt was enough to get Spider-Angela back upright, and she scuttled for the tunnel exit.

"LAVA. COMING!!!"

Rip stood dumbfounded as a huge hole appeared in the wall of the cave, and in poured a series of large, fiery-red lizard creatures. Blocky fireballs spewed from their mouths as they clambered along the walls and floor of the cave—right toward Ripley!

Ripley blinked, as if snapping out of a trance. He turned to follow Angela but one of the fire lizards was blocking the way out.

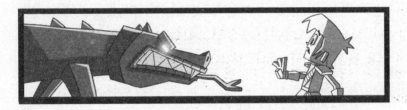

It belched fireballs in his direction, and Ripley had to leap to one side to avoid them.

With a feeling of dread, he realized he was surrounded. Ripley began to shake all over.

This was it.

It was going to be **GAME OVER**.

RIIIPP!
Up here!!

With a sudden flood of hope, Ripley followed the sound of the voice above. It was Mei!

"MEI!" he cried in relief. "I'm ... I'm stuck down here. I don't have a lot of time ..."

Mei hesitated. "I'll find a way to get you up. I will. I'm going to need to craft something. Give me a sec!"

Sinister reptilian hisses grew louder all around him as more lizards fixated their fiery gaze on Rip.

"Uh ... I don't have a sec, Mei! I need something to slow them down!"

Mei panicked and fumbled with her backpack. *Think, Mei. Think!*

She saw something shiny in her backpack—the medallion. It must be powerful, but she wasn't sure how to use it.

Then, she saw, or rather *smelled*, something she'd forgotten about. A faint cloud of rotten egg and stinky, moldy cheese smell reached her nostrils. Her fingers closed around the small, cube-like petals of the fart flower.

Not knowing what else to do, she stuck her head through the cavern hole and called out, "HEY! Try *this* while I craft something to get you out!"

The flower fluttered down and landed at Rip's feet. Ripley stared at it in disbelief. "A FLOWER?!"

"Not just any flower," she said, tapping her nose and grinning.

Rip had no other choice but to use Mei's stinky flower for protection. He snatched

the slightly withered bloom from the ground
and held it out toward the lizards.

Amazingly, he saw little stink lines radiating
from its pretty yellow blossom.
The stench was *awful*,
somehow amplified
by the heat. Ripley
coughed and
choked on the
horrible odor.

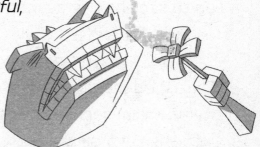

"Seriously, Mei, this
is gross. It's—" But he stopped, as he
watched one of the lizards recoil at the
horrible cloud of gas. "Hey!" He laughed. "It's
working!"

More of the fire lizards howled and
snarled before retreating too.

"I think I'm going to be OK!" he said
triumphantly.

A fiery ball of flames suddenly shot across
the cavern and engulfed the flower in his hand.

"Argh!" Ripley cried, dropping the smoldering flower. The flames had not reached his hand, but the fart flower was now a pile of ash on the ground. Rip looked up to see the fire beasts advancing. *Great.*

"Um, Mei . . . ?"

"Quick, Ripley!" Mei produced a rope ladder that she'd managed to craft from several items in her backpack. She lowered it down into the cave, securing the other end to a boulder in the upper cavern where she was waiting for him.

Without a moment's hesitation, Ripley reached for the ropes and began scrambling up the ladder.

Hissss!

Ripley could hear that one of the lizards was close. Before he could react, a fireball engulfed him! Ripley felt white-hot, burning heat all over, but, amazingly, no *actual* pain. His chest-armor had protected him!

Still, there was now smoke—the flames had reached the rope and were taking hold.

The ladder!

"Mei . . . the ladder is on fire!"

Lizard creatures were climbing the walls and moving onto the ceiling in an attempt to cut Rip off before he could escape.

"Climb *faster,* Ripley! I'll pull at the same time!"

Rip frantically climbed for the ceiling. Mei was hoisting the ladder with all her might, trying her best to pull Rip to safety—but he was too heavy. The fire lizards were closing in, and so was the fire.

"Rip, your armor—you've got to let it go. You're too heavy with it on!"

Rip panicked, swinging to avoid another fireball. Without his armor, he would be more

157

vulnerable. But with it, he might not be able
to escape!

"Rip—hurry. *PLEASE!!*"

There was no other option. With one last
burst of energy, Ripley managed to tear the
armor from his body and let it fall down onto
the seething group of angry lizards below.

One rope-ladder rung after another he
climbed, finally hauling himself up through the
ceiling hole and into the upper cavern.

But Rip and Mei weren't safe yet!

"We have to cover the hole with
something," Ripley panted, trying to catch his
breath. His skin still tingled with the heat
from below.

Mei looked around frantically, searching
the rocky surroundings. "There isn't anything.
We'll have to craft something."

Ripley almost laughed, and nodded. *Of
course!*

He opened up his backpack and pulled out
enough stone to build a sturdy hatch door,

and began assembling the pieces. It was complete in seconds.

He and Mei both lifted the stone hatch with all their might toward the hole—just as one of the fire lizards burst through!

HAIL MEGALAVA, LORD OF THE GAME!

A hot explosion of flames filled the upper cavern, narrowly missing them.

Rip and Mei exchanged glances.

"Who is this 'Lava' guy?!" Ripley wondered aloud, gripping the stone door tightly.

"MEGALAVA SEES ALL. RULES ALL. GAMERS COME. GAMERS NEVER LEAVE. LAVA WINS."

"Yeah, well. We're not just any gamers, fire-breath," Mei quipped, nodding at Ripley. Taking her cue, he nodded back, and they both hoisted the stone hatch in the direction of the lizard, forcing him back down into the hole. With an angry cry, the reptile stumbled backward in a cloud of smoke and flames.

"MEGALAVA WILL—"

But there was only silence as the stone hatch sealed the hole shut. Rip and Mei were alone in the darkness once more.

THE LAST STRETCH

Ripley and Mei's torches lit up the jagged walls around them as the two forged onward and upward, hoping to escape the mine before they discovered more trouble.

"We look terrible," said Mei. Her hair was covered in tiny cubes of dirt and rock, and she did her best to shake it out. Rip was pulling at the spider silk that was still stuck to his arms and legs.

"At least we have spider silk now!" said Rip, adding it to his bag.

"So, that fire lizard said there's something called Megalava ... What's that about?" Mei wondered as they walked along the winding path.

"Oh yeah, that was strange . . . Oh, Mei!" Rip exclaimed, tapping himself on the forehead. "I forgot to tell you, that giant spider down there—it was Angela!"

"What are you saying, Rip?" she replied.

"It was her. Actually her, in a new form. I saw her face. She was under the control of the game somehow. Also, I think she was going to eat me. Which was pretty intense."

Mei looked concerned. "That's . . . not good. Is she . . . stuck like that?" Mei's eyes grew wide. "Rip, we have to work out the rules of this game."

"Yeah, I know. Actually, I remember Angela said something about 'Big Lava,' and the fire lizard said Megalava. I wonder if they are the same thing. A game boss, maybe?"

"Maybe. And if Angela was destroyed by the night monsters, why didn't she just leave the game? And what will happen to us, if we . . . I mean, I thought that fire lizard was

just making stuff up to scare us, I didn't think it was TRUE," Mei said, worried.

"Hey, Mei, it's OK," said Rip. "Angela was careless. You and I are going to get through this game, and beat it, and then we'll see Angela out in the real world. Plus, you've got the medallion," Rip added. "That must do something special."

Mei pulled the medallion out of her bag. "This is important," she agreed. "I don't know why. But it is."

Mei put it back in her bag thoughtfully, and they continued to walk in silence for a while.

Mei saw it first. "There!" she said pointing upward at a large cube above them. "It's daylight!"

Someone or something had built a direct shaft down. A rookie mistake—you never build straight down. You can never get back out that way, which was now the exact problem Rip and Mei faced.

The entrance was very high up, but Mei could just make out a few tree branches hanging over the edges. It was the forest.

Mei said, "It's definitely our way out. But how do we get up there?"

Rip thought for a moment and said, "Digging a shaft system upward would take a long time. Maybe even a whole day."

"We don't have that kind of time," Mei replied. "This mine is dangerous, and I don't know how long that trapdoor will keep those fire lizards at bay."

They turned toward each other, seemingly having the same idea at the same time.

Rip pulled out his bow and began breaking it apart. He positioned wood cubes in a cross shape on the ground, and applied some silk strands to the shorter cross. *Shuunk.*

Ripley held up his new, spider-silk strengthened crossbow.

"Hopefully, arrows should go much farther now. And do more damage," he said.

"That's *perfect*!" Mei said. "Spider silk is one of the strongest materials in the world! Did you know spider legs move by using hydraulics? They use hydraulics to jump too! Some can jump fifty times their own length."

"Let's hope lizards can't jump that high," Rip said. "Also, can we not talk about spiders anymore?"

"Sure." Mei grinned as she reached into her backpack and fashioned a grappling hook out of vines, silk, and stone. It was sharp to touch, and the vine section was strong and stretchy. Mei passed the grappling hook to Rip.

"This grappling hook is *awesome*," Rip said with a grin. He placed the hook into the crossbow and wrapped a part of the silk vine around his arm. Mei did the same, and Rip aimed straight at the hole.

"Hold on!" he said.

Mei tightened her grip on the vine. "If you miss, I'm going to be very, very angry," she said.

"I never miss!"

Mei raised her eyebrows.

"OK, well, I sometimes miss," Rip said.

He pulled the trigger, and the hook shot straight up into the air, stretching the grapple vine until it was taut. The hook hit something, and they both felt it take hold.

There was a moment of hesitation, as if the tension of the vine and the forces of gravity were in a stalemate, working out what to do next. Then Mei and Rip were pulled upward toward the blue hole.

They were moving so fast, the sharp, blocky walls around them were a blur as they whizzed past. They approached the top, and the tension of the vine lessened, which

thankfully also reduced their speed. Rip and Mei shot through the opening into the air and straight into a tree. The bushy branches caught them, their arms and faces scratched by cube-shaped leaves.

"Ouch, ouch, ouch!" Rip yelled.

"Don't be a wuss!" Mei replied, spitting some leaves out of her mouth.

Ripley and Mei hung there in the branches for a moment, a little dazed and confused.

CRACK!

The tree split in half and dissolved into cubes, throwing Rip and Mei to the ground with a heavy thud.

"Ouch, ouch, ouch!" Mei yelled.

"Don't be a wuss!" Rip said, mockingly.

Mei poked out her tongue.

THUD!

They were inches away from the mineshaft opening. But they were out of the mine.

They were safe.

Rip and Mei slowly stood up, shaking off bits of dust and dirt out of their hair and clothes. It was midmorning, and there were no monsters to be seen. Right in front of them was Angela's fallen castle. They had barely moved!

Rip and Mei stood there, exhausted and hungry.

"That was quite a show!" said a familiar voice behind them.

Quite a show, indeed!

THE ANSWER

Sir Crabbington of Beachburry scuttled about in the pixelated grass, clicking with excitement when he came across a berry and promptly devouring it.

"Easy now, Sir Crabbington!" George said with a groan, laboriously climbing down from the crab's back, staff in hand. "He's had a big night. Definitely earned himself that new set of armor!" He gave the crab a friendly pat on the shell. "Terrified of butterflies, though. Very odd. So! I see you two are still alive! Very well done! Although I dare say, you look *terrible*!"

Mei and Rip did indeed look like they'd just barely survived a war. They were both covered in ash and mud, their clothes were

torn, and they had scrapes and bruises on their arms and legs. Mei was attempting to pull sticky clumps of spiderweb out of her tangled hair.

"*We're* alive? What about *you*? The last time we saw you, you were about to battle a pack of monsters!" Mei said.

"You know," Rip added, a little annoyed, "you could have warned us about all of this!"

"Didn't I? Ha! Deary me. Terribly sorry. I thought I was quite brave, actually, coming to your rescue earlier. Well—how's this for a warning. You had better eat something!"

Mei looked down at the one heart left on her wristband. Keeping track of health was hard!

The two adventurers hurriedly dug around inside their packs for some food.

"All I have is fish," Mei said.

"Me too," Rip sighed. "Should I make a fire?"

The last half a heart on Rip's wristband was blinking rapidly. His entire body was starting to turn slightly translucent.

"Rip, you're literally fading away!" Mei exclaimed in alarm. "No time for a fire—just *eat*!"

The raw fish was cold and scaly, and tasted horribly fishy. It was not a pleasant meal to be having after all they'd been through. Mei found herself wondering why the carrots had tasted so bland, and yet the flavor of raw fish in her mouth was so strong—that hardly seemed fair!

Begrudgingly, she ate just enough to see her heart meter filling back up again, then slumped down on the ground. Rip was starting to look decidedly more opaque.

"OK, so ask me anything," said George.

Rip and Mei looked at each other. Rip shrugged his shoulders. "Where do we start?" he said.

Mei's mind was starting to work properly

again and she thought about moments in games where there was a chance to ask questions—by working out what the most important question was, the gamer could get an advantage. Even though she wanted to know about what happened to Angela and so many other things, she tried to think what was THE most important thing of all . . .

"I just want to go home. Please, George. Can you just tell us how to get OUT of here?" Mei asked.

George smiled warmly. "Well, of COURSE I can! Silly girl—you only had to ask!"

She leapt back up, grabbing Rip's arm excitedly.

"WELL?" Rip said. "What do we have to do?"

George stroked his beard thoughtfully. "I can help you, but KNOW THIS: I can only give you this answer for free—*once*. After that, a price must be paid."

Rip shrugged. "Who cares? Once we're out of here we won't need your help again anyway!"

Mei laughed with relief and exhaustion. They were so close! She could practically feel the warmth of her own bed and smell the enticing aroma of her mother's cooking. She wanted to go home more than anything else in the world right now.

George regarded them both with a strange look in his eye. "Very well, then. To leave this world, you need only to walk through the right door."

Rip and Mei exchanged glances.

"Door?" Mei asked urgently. "What *door*?!"

"The answer can only be crafted. But it must be done at a place of great power."

George lifted a gnarled finger and pointed off into the distance. Rip and Mei looked where George was pointing and saw an outcrop of rocks on a small hilltop. It was glowing a soft purple.

"So ... we craft this ... 'door' ... at the

place of power. And that will get us out of here?" Rip asked, uncertain.

The wizard nodded solemnly.

Rip and Mei studied the hilltop, curious as to what kind of magic was radiating from within.

Rip gathered his courage and looked determined. "OK. We'll do it. Honestly, this game . . . it's been . . . insane. We've never played anything like it! We encountered another player—Angela. She'd been turned into some kind of spider! We *need* to find—"

Rip and Mei turned back around. But George the Wizard was gone.

The two gamers approached the hill. Storm clouds seemed to gather over just this part of the landscape, churning and crackling with electricity. A strange tingling sensation rippled across Mei's skin. She looked down

to find her arms were covered in goose bumps.

"Do you think . . . this is . . . what magic feels like?" Mei asked.

Rip shivered. "I guess so. I'm a little nervous. This place kind of gives me the creeps."

The climb was long and exhausting. Occasionally they had to stop and help each other up some particularly steep rock faces, removing their packs and passing the bags between them to get over tricky sections of the jagged, pixelated ascent.

At last, however, they reached the summit. The magical storm intensified. Wind howled around them, and rain began to fall in heavy sheets. Rip and Mei grabbed on to each other for support.

"I feel like I'm going to get blown away!" Rip yelled over the raging weather.

"Let's just get this done," Mei yelled back, wet hair slick against her face and rain

pelting into her eyes. "We're so close to freedom, Rip!"

Rip nodded, pulling his own hair from his eyes and turning his attention to their final task. There didn't seem to be any obvious place to build a door—no cave or opening for them to walk through. It was just a sharp collection of rocks with a level area in the center.

The purple, magical energy pulsated from within the rock, casting a shimmering haze through the waterfall of rain.

"Where do we start?" Rip wondered, exasperated.

Mei thought for a moment. "Maybe . . . it isn't so much of a door that we need, but . . . a portal!"

Rip snapped his fingers. "Yes! A portal that will transport us back into the real world! What do you need to build portals out of?"

Mei shook her head, her mind racing. "I—I don't know. It's different in every game."

"Well . . . we have the diamond we collected from the mine . . ." Rip suggested, eyes hopeful.

Mei looked unconvinced. "I don't think diamond has any magical properties—it's just really strong. I've never heard of portals being built out of diamond."

"Well . . ." Rip threw his hands up in the air. "We have to try something!"

Lightning crackled amid the dark purple clouds above them. Mei nodded and yelled again over the roar of the storm, "You're right. Let's just try it!"

They started pulling cubes of the diamond they'd collected from their packs and setting them down in piles on the flat surface of the magic hilltop.

"Rip—*look!*" Mei shouted excitedly, pointing to their pile.

Rip hefted the last cube of diamond from his pack and turned to look at the pile they'd

amassed. But it was no longer a pile of pale, shimmering diamond blocks. They now glittered and shone a brilliant purple, shot through with flashes of rainbow light.

In his hands, the final block of diamond remained in its original state, but as soon as he placed it on the surface of the mountain, it too transformed into this new material.

"It's the magic coming from this rock!" Rip realized aloud. "When combined with diamond, it changes the material into something else!"

Mei watched the dancing flashes of rainbow and purple light. "It's . . . beautiful. What do you think it is?"

Rip shrugged. "No idea. But it must be what we need to build the portal. Why else would George have told us to build it here?"

Mei didn't need any more convincing. She raced over to the gem pile and began stacking the blocks on top of one another. Rip helped her to build the structure so that it stood taller than they did, using regular stone to frame the outside of the shimmering doorway. As Rip placed the last framing stone, encasing the purple crystal within, the structural integrity of the creation began to shift.

"Mei, step back," Rip warned. "Something's happening."

They both backed away, drenched from the rain, tired from all the heavy lifting, but filled with excitement. The wind seemed to whirl and twist with even more force, the sky a boiling sea of angry clouds and electrical energy.

The bright purple stone in the center of the portal shimmered and changed, suddenly turning into a mirrored surface. They saw themselves for the first time in what seemed like forever,

staring at their reflections, battered, bruised, standing in the storm.

Mei took a step forward. "Shall we . . . try it together?"

A smile spread across Rip's face. "Together," he agreed.

He held out his hand and Mei took it firmly.

"Mei . . . ?" Rip said, looking across at his companion. "You're a pretty decent gamer."

Mei grinned, no longer bothered by the rain. "You're not so bad yourself."

LOADING...

Mei looked inside her own backpack. "I still have the medallion," she said, holding up the strange bronze object they had pulled from the mine. "What does it do?"

They both inspected the medallion. It had some unusual carvings, which made it look like it connected to a bigger piece.

Rip and Mei were starting to panic a little. Rip wondered if they would ever escape this game or if they were lost in it forever.

Would that be so bad?

Then he thought of the number of times they'd already both come close to death. He decided that yes, this was exciting, but he was ready to go home. Besides, who would want to play the same game forever, even if it was great?

"What's that?" asked Mei, pointing behind Rip to a small hole hovering in the white. "There!"

They both moved toward the strange hole.
It was just sitting there, not attached to
anything. Mei looked at the medallion, at the
hole, and then to Rip.

CLICK

The medallion fit perfectly. Mei turned it until it locked into place.

CLICK CLICK CLICK

A trumpet fanfare sounded.

LEVEL ONE: DIG WORLD COMPLETE!

Rip and Mei smiled. Maybe it really was over.

ENTERING LEVEL TWO!

There was a loud crack and then they were falling through the air again. Down and down they tumbled, the world around them slowly taking shape as it loaded in. The white became blue and then dark blue and then filled with clouds.

"Whoa, these cloud graphics are great! Look at those textures! So detailed!" yelled Rip.

Immediately it became very clear that they were not heading home. Mei took in a sharp breath.

It was an entire army of dragons, soaring over the land below in magnificent formation. Mei had always loved the *idea* of dragons, but now she was about to have a very close encounter with one!

They were falling—and *fast*. Rip realized this too, and his body tensed to brace for impact.

THUMP

Rip and Mei crashed onto the back of a green dragon, both scrambling to grab hold of it. Rip managed to spread his arms out over the back of the beast in a terrifying airborne hug of sorts.

Mei bounced and was able to land her legs directly on the beast's long neck. They felt the dragon's body flinch in surprise at the sudden addition of two passengers, and it let out a mighty, terrifying bellow.

The portal had not taken them home at all.

Rip and Mei were riding a real, fire-breathing, razor-toothed dragon. They were moving with intense speed, the rhythmic beating of the dragon's wings propelling them sharply through the air. Rip managed to raise his head just enough to get a glimpse of where they were headed.

The wind stung his eyes. Hundreds of tiny airborne figures dotted the horizon ... *more dragons*?

There was another, angry bellow—which was promptly echoed by all the other dragons in their flying formation.

"Rip! What is *happening*?!" Mei cried.

Rip's eyes were fixed on the horizon. Their army of dragons was about to collide head-on with another, larger group of black dragons.

"Oh no ..." Ripley swallowed, gripping the green dragon's back more tightly. "I think we're going to war ... with dragons."